12/91

THE HIGH GRADERS

THE HIGH GRADERS

LOUIS L'AMOUR

BANTAM BOOKS

NEW YORK · TORONTO · LONDON · SYDNEY

THE HIGH GRADERS
A Bantam Book

PRINTING HISTORY
Bantam paperback edition / January 1965
Louis L'Amour hardcover edition / April 1985

Book design by Renée Gelman

ISBN 0-553-06273-5

Published simultaneously in the United States and Canada

Bantam Books are published by Bantam Books, a division of
Bantam Doubleday Dell Publishing Group, Inc. Its trademark,
consisting of the words "Bantam Books" and the portrayal of a
rooster, is Registered in U.S. Patent and Trademark Office and in
other countries. Marca Registrada. Bantam Books, 666 Fifth
Avenue, New York, New York 10103.

PRINTED IN THE UNITED STATES OF AMERICA

10 9 8 7 6 5 4 3 2

THE HIGH GRADERS

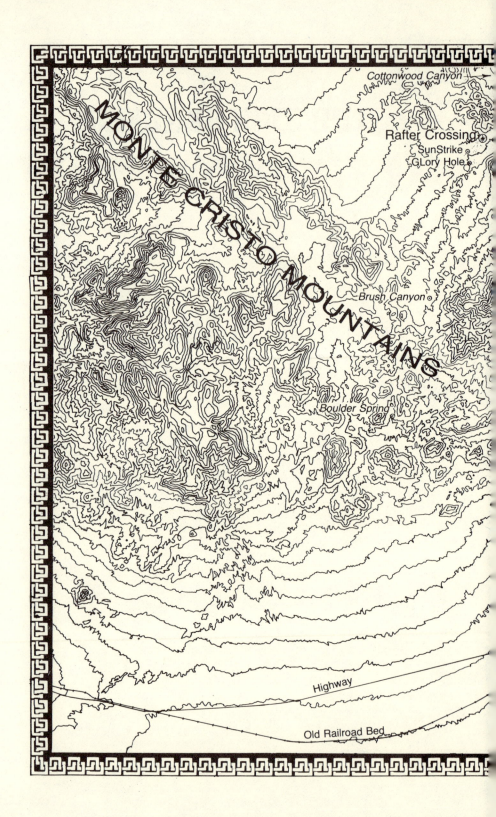

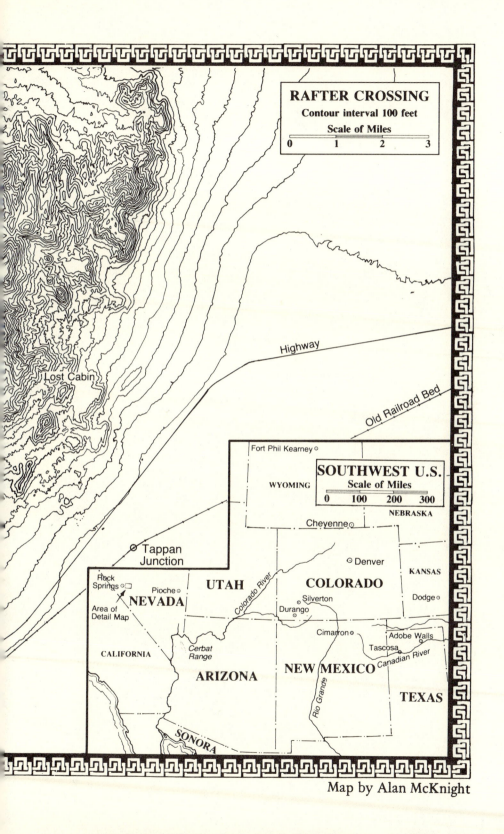

RAFTER CROSSING
Contour interval 100 feet
Scale of Miles
0   1   2   3

Highway

Old Railroad Bed

Lost Cabin

Fort Phil Kearney ○

SOUTHWEST U.S.
Scale of Miles
0   100   200   300

WYOMING

NEBRASKA

Cheyenne ○

⊘ Tappan
Junction

○ Denver

KANSAS

Rock
Springs ○▯

Pioche ○

UTAH

Colorado River

COLORADO

Dodge ○

NEVADA

Silverton ○

Durango ○

Area of
Detail Map

CALIFORNIA

Cerbat
Range

Cimarron ○

Adobe Walls ○

Tascosa ○

ARIZONA

NEW MEXICO

Canadian River

Rio Grande

TEXAS

SONORA

Map by Alan McKnight

ONE

Mike Shevlin squatted on his heels in the driving rain and struck a match under the shelter of his slicker. The match flared and he leaned forward, cupping the flame in his hand against the face of the gravestone.

ELI PATTERSON
1811–1876

There was no mistake, then; but how in the name of truth could a peace-loving man like old Eli wind up in a grave on Boot Hill?

Eli Patterson had been a Quaker, a man of deep conviction who never touched a gun for his own use and did not approve of those who did. Yet he was dead, shot to death, and buried here among the victims of gun and knife, and if rumor could be credited, he had himself died gun in hand.

The flame flickered out and the dropped match hissed against the sodden earth. "Anybody but him," Shevlin said aloud; "anybody but old Eli."

The splash of a footstep in a pool of water warned him an instant before the voice spoke. "Kind of wet up here, isn't it?"

Mike Shevlin straightened slowly to his feet, glad his slicker was unbuttoned and his gun ready to hand. Enemies he would surely find at Rafter Crossing, but he could expect no friends. He took his time in facing around, careful that his movements be not misunderstood.

Through the pouring rain and the darkness he could see the bulk of a square, powerfully built man. Lightning flared, throwing the grave crosses into sharp relief, lighting the water-

1

soaked earth, and making an occasional gleam on stone, but of the wide face before him he could make out no detail.

The other man would see even less of Shevlin, because of the up-turned collar of his slicker and the pulled-down brim of his black hat.

"You make a practice of following people?" Mike Shevlin asked.

"It's a wet night to be on Boot Hill."

"I've buried men here on wetter nights. If need be I can bury more."

"Ah, I was right then. You're no stranger." There was satisfaction in the man's voice. Lightning glinted off the badge on his chest.

Mike Shevlin put a rein to his tongue. This was no bumbling old Sheriff McKown, nor anybody he remembered from the Rafter Crossing he had known. Wanting no trouble, he simply said, "I've been here before, if that's what you mean."

The man with the badge shifted his feet slightly. "Are you Ray Hollister?"

"If you don't know Ray Hollister," Shevlin replied, "you haven't been around long."

"Two years. He left before I came."

Shevlin had an uneasy feeling that had he said he was Ray Hollister, the sheriff would have killed him.

Wind and rain lashed the grave-covered knoll, whipping the branches of the trees. Off to the right were the lights of the town—many more lights than he remembered. Beyond the town was the gallows frame and the huddled buildings of a mine, lighted for a night shift.

"Too wet to talk here," Shevlin said. "What's on your mind?"

"You were looking at Patterson's grave. He was killed in a gun battle two years ago."

Anger flared up in Mike Shevlin. "Whoever told you that," he said roughly, "lied."

"Then the coroner lied, Mason lied, and Gib Gentry lied."

"Who killed him?"

"Gentry—in self-defense. Mason was a witness. Patterson still had a gun in his hand when others came up."

Suddenly Shevlin knew he was not likely to be offered a drink nor a hot meal on this night. Rain slanted across the windows down there in town, windows behind which it would be dry and warm, but where he might be identified before he found out what he had come so far to learn.

Gentry? No, not for a minute. Not Gib. Gib would shoot fast enough, but he would never have shot Eli Patterson.

"No coroner's jury in the old times would believe that story. They knew Eli too well."

Shevlin, who knew most things that might be expected at a time like this, was prepared for the match when it flared in the sheriff's hand, and his own hand was suddenly before his face, pulling down his hat brim. The flare revealed only the sheriff's own tough, weather-beaten features.

Now where had he seen *that* face before?

"The old-timers are gone, or most of them," the man said. "Times have changed. Why don't you ride on?"

"Why should I?"

There was irritation in the sheriff's response to this. "Because you smell of trouble, and trouble is my business. You start anything and I'll have to come against you."

"Thanks." Shevlin's tone was dry, harsh. "You've warned me, now I'll return the favor. Don't make my trouble your business, and don't come against me."

The sheriff gestured across the valley at the huddle of mine buildings. "They tell me that's where the old Rafter H headquarters used to be. Now they use the old barn as a hoisthouse for the Sun Strike Mine. That's just one indication. This town is no longer cattle, my friend, it's mining. You won't find anybody around who knows you, and nobody who wants you here. Do yourself a favor and ride on."

Mike Shevlin, who had known many men, knew this was a truly dangerous man. He knew it because the sheriff had not tried to force the issue, as a less experienced man might have done; knew it because he was calm, talking quietly, trying to avoid trouble before it arrived, and because he was so obviously one of those who knew when and when not to use a gun.

The two men walked together toward the gate and Shevlin closed it carefully behind him, then swept the water from his saddle with a flick of his palm. He gathered the reins and turned his horse so he could mount without showing his back to the sheriff. The latter noted the move with grim appreciation, and mounted his own horse.

Just as Shevlin had learned much of the sheriff in these few minutes, so the sheriff had learned something of the man who loomed only as a dark figure on a rain-swept hill. There was a hard sureness about this stranger, and he allowed for no chances against him, and there was also a confidence in him that warned the sheriff this man who faced him was no outlaw, that it was even likely he had himself carried a badge.

"I'll tell you something." Mike Shevlin, who normally explained his actions to no man, explained them now in deference to the kind of man this was. "In my lifetime one man gave me a square shake without figuring to get something out of it. That man was Eli Patterson."

There was a pause.

"You'll be staying on, then?" the sheriff asked.

"I'll be staying."

The sheriff tried again. "Look," he said patiently, "you start shaking the brush to find what happened to Eli Patterson and you'll have the whole town on you."

Mike Shevlin turned his horse toward Main Street. Over his shoulder he said, "It's a small town."

As he rode away he told himself he was a fool. He should not have come back. What could any man do to help the dead?

He had returned because a fine old man who had been his friend when he had no friends had been murdered, and his killers had gone unpunished. Nor could that one murder have made an end to it, for the wicked do not cease from wickedness, nor does evil end with one crime.

The rain beat a hard tattoo upon his hat as he walked his black along the street. From the rain-whipped darkness he peered into the lighted windows as he passed, windows of houses where he was a stranger, and past doors where he would not be welcomed. If he slept in a bed this night it would be a bed he paid for, and if he ate at all it would be a meal he bought for cash.

He drew rein in the muddy street, feeling the cold rain hammering his shoulders with cruel fingers. Saddle-worn and weary from the long riding, he stared into the windows and knew again that pang of loneliness with which he always rode.

There was welcome for him nowhere, neither in this place nor anywhere down along the trail. Only that kind old man lying in a shameful grave had been considerate, kind to a skinny, hollow-eyed boy who had walked into his store so long ago, carrying little but a man-sized pride.

Because of this he had ridden a thousand hot, dangerous miles, returning to a town he remembered without pleasure, to seek out the cause of an old man's death and to clear his name so that his spirit might rest easy in the earth.

So Ray Hollister was gone. The town would not be the same without him, but obviously the town did not want him back. Not, at least, that part of the town represented by the sheriff.

That the town of Rafter Crossing did not like Ray Hollister, Mike Shevlin could understand. He himself had never liked the man, for Hollister was a man with a burr under his saddle, a small rancher who wanted to be big, who strode hard-heeled around the town, wanting to be considered one of the big cattlemen who ruled the destinies of the Rafter country. Nothing in Hollister's character nor in the breadth of his acres entitled him to the respect he wanted so desperately, and his envy and irritation became a bitter, gnawing thing within him.

Mike Shevlin turned in his saddle, looking along the wet street. Three blocks long when he had left it, with two saloons, it was seven blocks long now, with at least six saloons on the one street. The old Hooker House had become the Nevada House, and had a fresh coat of paint. There was an assay office where the harness shop had been, and a new general store across from the one Eli Patterson had owned.

Windows threw rectangles of light across the muddy street, and the sound of a tin-panny piano came from the direction of the Nevada House. Thunder rumbled in the mountains. Shevlin started his horse, staring morosely at the lights as he rode on.

His mind went to the past. Everything here had changed, and not even the memory of the way it had been was left to him. It was indeed a mining town now; not a vestige of the old cow town remained.

His thoughts reverted to Eli Patterson. They said Gib Gentry had killed him, but not for an instant did he believe that. The fact that Mason was a witness proved nothing, for Mason had been a liar as well as a petty thief.

Gib Gentry and Shevlin had been friends . . . or what passed as such. They had worked together, ridden into town together, been in trouble together. Despite that, there had been no real affection between them; they had simply been thrown together as two people are, held together by work and mutual associations, and considered by everyone to be friends. And both had done foolish things.

"You should have had your ears slapped down," Shevlin told himself.

The trouble was that nobody around Rafter had wanted to tackle that job, not even then. Now he was thirty years old and the veteran of more gun trouble than he cared to remember.

In the old days Gentry and Shevlin had seemed to be two of a kind, reckless and wild, full of ginger, and homeless as a pair of tumbleweeds. Ready to fight at the drop of a hat, and to drop the hat themselves if need be. And Gentry had been good with a gun.

He had been better with a gun than Shevlin in those days. He was eight years older, and had owned a gun that much longer and had had that much more practice. But a lot of water had flowed under the bridge since then, and a lot had happened to Mike Shevlin that could never happen to Gib Gentry in Rafter Crossing. In the words of the cow country, Mike Shevlin had been up the creek and over the mountain since then.

The rain lashed his face, driven by the rising wind. This was the story of his life, he thought bitterly—hunting a place to hole up for a while. Thirty years old, and nothing to show for it but a horse, a saddle, and a couple of guns.

He was riding past the last of the town's buildings when he remembered the old mill in Brush Canyon. It might have been torn down for the lumber, or burned in some brush fire, but if it was still there it would be shelter from the storm and from observation. The mill had been old, even in his time, mute evidence of a dream that dried up when the water did. It was unlikely that newcomers would know of its existence.

With no better place to go, he turned into the trail around the livery barn and started up the slant of the hill in the driving rain. Brush whipped at his slicker and at his face, but he bowed his head and kept on.

From the crest of the ridge he looked back upon the town's lights. If he had been a smart man, he thought, he would now own a ranch or a business of some kind, but he had never known any way of doing what had to be done than to bull in and start swinging.

At the bottom of Brush Canyon he detected a subtle alteration in the manner of his horse, and like any western rider in wild country he had learned to depend on the instincts as well as on the sight and hearing of his horse, to know its moods, to be aware of every change of muscle or movement. Stepping down now from the saddle, Shevlin explored the muddy trail with careful fingers.

What he found was the indentation of a hoof track so recent as to be easily discernible in spite of the rain. That track had probably been made within the last few minutes.

Wiping the mud from his hand on the horse's mane, he walked the horse past the dark bulk of the old mill and dismounted at the stable. Here he led the horse inside, closed the door behind him, and struck a match.

On each side of the barn there were a dozen stalls, for it was here they had kept the big Clydesdales used to haul logs to the mill, and to haul away the planks. There were four horses in the stable now, and they rolled their eyes around to look at him.

He led his mount to a vacant stall, touching each horse as he passed. Two were dry, one was slightly damp, and the fourth was as wet as his own. Two riders, then, had been here most of the day, the others arriving since the rain began, and one of them only minutes before.

Stripping the rig from his black, he wiped the horse down with a dry sack he found hanging over the side of the stall. Come what might, he was through traveling for tonight. Then he checked the other horses.

The first was a cowhorse, the sort to be found in any remuda, and it wore a Turkeytrack brand, the old Moorman outfit. The fine dapple-gray mare was a Three Sevens. Obviously this was a woman's horse, for few cattlemen would ride anything but a gelding. The two geldings in the stable were both branded Open AV, a brand unfamiliar to Shevlin.

He struck a match and checked the droppings on the floor. The cowhorse and one of the geldings had been stabled here since the previous day, but there was no evidence that prior to that a horse had been here in months. So this was a meeting place, and not a permanent setup.

He stepped outside, moving quietly as was his usual way, and closed the door softly behind him. His attention was immediately riveted on a strange glisten of reflected light outside the mill's boarded window. With one hand resting on the corner of the barn, he carefully unfastened his slicker with the other.

What he saw was the shine of light on a rain-wet slicker like his own. Somebody was standing in the darkness near the mill door, waiting.

Drawing his gun, Shevlin waited for a flash of lightning. Poised as he was, the slight advantage was his when the shadows were suddenly broken by the lightning's glare. The other man shot too quickly, the bullet tearing the wood at the barn's corner within inches of Shevlin's hand.

Instantly, at the flash of the other man's gun, Shevlin fired in return.

The man fell hard against the side of the building, and his pistol splashed in the water; then he straightened with a grunt and ran, staggering, into the woods. A moment later Shevlin heard the pound of hoofs, and after that all was darkness and silence, with only the sound of the falling rain.

Shevlin walked to where the gun had fallen, and after a minute or two of groping he found it.

The tiny slit of light that had warned him of the watcher's presence was gone, but the door was open a crack and a rifle muzzle covered him.

"Hold it right there, mister," a voice said, "and holster that gun."

Shevlin tucked the .45 behind his belt, trying to place the voice, which seemed familiar. He walked toward the door, saying conversationally, "We had better talk this over in the light, *amigo*. There was a time when I knew Turkeytrack mighty well."

"Hold up there!"

No stranger to the tone of a voice behind a gun, Mike Shevlin stopped.

"Who'd you ever know at Turkeytrack?" came the question from the darkness.

"Rawhide Jenkins was foreman then, and they had a sour-dough cook named Lemmon." Then the remembrance of the voice came to him suddenly, by association. "And they had a cantankerous old devil of a wolfer named Winkler."

The door opened wider. "Come on careful, with your hands empty."

"That wolf-hunter," Shevlin continued, "took over as cook one time when Lemmon was laid up. He made the best coffee and the lousiest biscuits a man ever ate."

He walked up the ramp and into the darkness of a room that had once been the main part of the sawmill. A fire glowed redly on a hearth across the room, and the firelight gleamed from the blade of the saw.

Shevlin paused just inside the door, his senses alert and waiting, his hands gripping lightly the edges of his slicker.

"Light it, Eve."

A match flared, revealing the face of a girl, strangely lovely in the soft light. She touched the flame to the wick of a coal-oil lantern, then lowered the globe and hung the lantern so the light fell upon Shevlin's face.

He knew what they saw: a big man with wide shoulders and a lean body that bulked even larger now with the wet slicker and the black leather chaps. A man over six feet tall who did not look the two hundred pounds he weighed, a man with a wedge-shaped face turned to leather by wind and sun.

Using his left hand, Shevlin tilted his hat back so they could see his face, wondering if the years had left enough for Winkler to recognize.

"Shevlin!" the man exclaimed. "Mike Shevlin! Well, I'll be dogged! Heard you was killed down on the Nueces."

"It was a close thing."

Winkler did not lower the rifle, and Shevlin held his peace, knowing why it covered him.

"What happened out there just now?"

"You had an eavesdropper. He tried a shot at me."

The huge room was almost empty. Here where the great saw blade had screamed through logs, cutting out planks to build the town, all was silent but for the subdued crackle of the fire and the rain on the walls and windows. The firelight and the lantern shed their glow even to the corners; he saw only the girl and the old wolfer, yet there had been four horses out there.

There were no chairs and no table, but there was a sixteen-foot pine log from which the top had been cut for planks, leaving a flat surface that was at once a bench and a table. Near the fireplace there was a stack of wood, and at the fire's edge an ancient, smoke-blackened coffeepot.

The girl was young, not much over twenty, but her manner was cool and carried authority. She regarded him with direct attention. "Do you always shoot that quick?"

"I take notions."

Winkler was still suspicious. "What did you come back for? Who sent for you?"

Removing his slicker, Shevlin walked to the fire and stretched his hands toward the coals. What was going on here? He had returned, it seemed, to a town crawling with suspicion and fear. How could mining do that to a town? Or was it the mining?

"What did you come back for?" Winkler repeated.

"Eli's dead."

"Eli?"

"Eli Patterson."

"That's been a while. Anyway, what's that to do with you? I never heard of you going out of your way for anybody. What did you have to do with that old coot?"

"I liked him." Shevlin rubbed his hands above the coals. "I've been down Sonora way. Only heard a few weeks ago that he was dead."

"So you came runnin', hey? Take my advice and light a shuck out of here. Everything's changed, and we've trouble enough without you."

"I want to know what happened to Eli."

Winkler snorted. "As I recall, he wasn't the man to do business with a cow thief."

Mike Shevlin had expected that, sooner or later. "Maybe he didn't think of me that way," he said mildly.

The girl spoke up. "Who sent you to this mill?" she asked.

"It seemed like a good place to sleep. Never dreamed anybody would be holed up here."

She must be Three Sevens. What did he know of the
Three Sevens outfit?

"You had friends here," Winkler said. "Why not go to them?
Or stop in the hotel?"

"I never had any friends in this country. Only Eli Patterson."

"You trailed with Gentry and them. What about him? What
about Ben Stowe?"

Rain drummed on the roof, but Shevlin was sure he heard a
faint stirring in the loft above. So that was where they were,
then.

"I think," Eve said, "that this man is a spy."

"You think whatever you're of a mind to. I'm going to get me
some sleep here." Then he added, "Eli gave me a job when I
was a youngster."

"He never owned no cattle," Winkler said.

"He hired me to unload a wagon for him, then he spoke to
Moorman about me: That's how come I hired on at Turkeytrack."

"You ran with Gentry and that crowd," Eve said. "I know all
about you."

"Who ever knows all about anybody? As to the Gentry
crowd, I'll own to having been my share of a fool."

Come to think of it, he had never been much of anything
else. He was a drifter, a man who fought for wages, mainly
because he knew how to do it better than most, even in this
country. Yet what did that mean? It meant when he was
through they paid him off, and were glad to be rid of him. And
in the end? In the end he would die up a canyon some place
when his ammunition gave out. Or at the end of a rope.

Weariness swept over him, and he felt empty, exhausted
both mentally and physically. He was tired of being wary, tired
of running, tired of being alert for trouble. But he could not
have picked a worse time to feel that way, for he had come
back to a country that was obviously on the brink of a shooting
war.

Yet he had no idea what was going on. He only knew that
the town was cold, wet, and unfriendly, just as it had been
seventeen years ago.

TWO

He had come to Rafter a gaunt youngster of thirteen astride a buckskin that showed every rib, thin as a bed slat himself, and wearing all he owned.

He carried a single-shot Sharps .50 buffalo gun, one ragged blanket, and a Navy Colt. The saddle he bestrode was a cast-off McClellan, left behind by the Army.

Eli Patterson had been alone in the store when the boy entered, wet to the skin, but carrying all the fine, stiff pride of a boy alone and seeking a man's job. A boy who was ragged and wet, and who knew he was nothing much to begin with.

"Know where a man can find work?" He was shaking with chill, but he fought the tremble from his voice.

"Need help myself," Patterson had lied. "Cold makes me stiff. There's a wagonload of stuff out back that needs unloading."

"I'm hunting a riding job," the boy said proudly, holding himself tall.

Patterson shrugged. "Take it or leave it."

Pride fought with hunger, and lost. "I'll take it," the boy said, "but if anybody asks you, I'm a rider, not no day hand."

Patterson nodded, and taking a silver dollar from his pocket, he said, "Dinnertime. You eat up and come back."

The half-starved youngster had looked at the old man with cold eyes. "I ain't earned it. I'll eat after."

Later in the day Jack Moorman walked into the store, tough, hearty old Jack. Eli nodded to indicate the boy. "Friend of mine, Jack, just rode in. I don't reckon he's really rustling work, but if you need a hand, he's a rider."

Moorman turned his head to look, taking in the story at a glance. He was a bluff, kindly man. "Can you ride bog, boy?" he asked.

"Yes, sir. And I can rope an' tie, and I've got the best cuttin'
horse in this here country." He gestured toward the sorry-
looking buckskin at the hitch rack.

"That crow-bait?" Moorman scoffed. "Why, I wouldn't have
that rack of bones on the place!"

"Keep your job then," Mike Shevlin replied brusquely. "I'll
not work for a man who judges a horse by the meat on him."

Surprised, Jack Moorman glanced around at Eli as if to say,
'Hey, what is this?' Then he said, "Sorry, son, no offense
intended. You just come on out and bring your horse. I sur-
mise all he needs is a bait or two of oats and some grama."

Following that meeting with Jack Moorman, Mike Shevlin
had worked two years for Turkeytrack, filling out and growing
taller. And no man in the outfit had shouldered extra work
because he was a boy, nor had Mike backed away from trouble.
Not even on the day when he rode up to a rustler with a
tied-down Turkeytrack calf and a brand half altered.

Old Jack came out to the horse camp to hear Mike's account
of the shooting, for the rustler had been brought to headquarters draped over a saddle. Moorman saw the burn on the boy's
arm from a bullet that just missed.

"He told me to take out runnin' and to keep my trap shut
about things that didn't concern me. Said I'd live a lot longer. I
told him I rode for the brand, and rustlin' Turkeytrack stock
concerned me a-plenty.

"He grabbed for his gun, only I taken my time and he didn't.
He got off the first shot, and he missed."

"Boy"—Moorman shifted his big body in the saddle—"you
wore that gun when I first saw you, and I figured you were
young for it, but you've worked two years for me and this is the
first time you've ever dragged iron. You're old enough to wear
a gun, all right."

At fifteen Mike Shevlin was as tall as he ever would be, and
was stronger than most men. He had never known a day of
anything but hard work, and was proud that he could work beside
men and hold their respect.

From ten to thirteen he had worked beside his uncle on a
mining claim, taking his regular turn with single-jack or double-
jack. Swinging the heavy sledges had put power in his shoulders and had taught him to hit with his weight behind it.

As a result, when Turkeytrack rode over to the dances at
Rock Springs schoolhouse, or over to Horse Hollow, Mike
Shevlin won six fist fights before losing one. And he whipped
that man the following Saturday night.

When he rode away from the Moorman outfit and started

running with Gib Gentry and Ben Stowe, Eli Patterson warned him against it. "They're a bad crowd, Mike. They're not your kind."

Now, listening to the rain outside the old mill, he knew again, as he had realized long before, that Eli Patterson had been right. Gentry and Stowe had always run with the wrong crowd; a man is judged by the company he keeps, and so had Mike Shevlin been judged.

"That old man should never have been buried on Boot Hill," he said. "To him, that would seem the final disgrace. I intend to find out what happened."

"Ask your friend Gentry," Eve said.

"You take my advice," Winkler said, "and you'll light out as soon as the rain lets up. You take out while you're able."

Shevlin turned his eyes to the girl. "I didn't get your name."

"Eve Bancroft. I own the Three Sevens."

But Winkler was not to be sidetracked. "You get out," he said. "I remember you, Shevlin, and that crowd you trailed with, and I've heard of you since, and none of it any good. You leave out of here or we'll bury you here."

Ignoring the old man, Shevlin rinsed a cup and filled it with coffee. His own cup was among the gear of his saddle.

These were cattle people. But the buildings in town were all mining—assay offices, miners' supplies, even the saloons now had names reflecting the mining business. So why were these people from the cattle ranches meeting here in secret?

Mike Shevlin's life had been lived in an atmosphere of range feuds and cattle wars, and this meeting had all the earmarks of a preliminary to such trouble. Why else would a pretty young woman like Eve Bancroft, a ranch owner, be meeting here with an old hard-case like Winkler, and whoever it was that was hiding upstairs?

He gulped the hot, strong coffee. "I'll bunk in the loft," he said, "and stay out of your way."

He finished the coffee and set down the cup; then he walked over to the ladder. Putting his hand on the rung to start climbing, he felt the dampness of wet mud under his fingers. Somebody was up there, all right, and waiting for him.

Eve started to speak, but hesitated; Winkler just watched him, his hard old eyes revealing nothing.

Shevlin climbed the ladder and lifted the trap with his left hand. Light shone suddenly in his eyes, but he spoke casually. "You pull that trigger, Ray, and you're a bigger fool than I thought."

He pushed the loose trap door aside, then went up through

the hole and kicked the trap shut without taking his eyes from the two men who waited there for him.

Ray Hollister looked older than he should have, and thinner than Shevlin remembered him. There was bitterness and frustration in the lines around his eyes and mouth, lines that Shevlin did not remember. Ray Hollister had found himself to be a smaller man than he wished to believe, and he hated it.

The other man, Babcock, was a thin, patient man of few loyalties, but they were loyalties grimly held. He believed in Ray Hollister and he believed in cattle; and of the two men, Shevlin was sure Babcock was the more dangerous—an impression that would have both surprised and infuriated Ray Hollister.

"Who told you I was here?" Hollister demanded. "Was it Eve?"

"They were expecting you in town, so when I saw four horses in the stable and realized somebody was hiding here, I knew it simply had to be you."

"I'm not hiding! I'll be damned if I am!"

"Who'd you shoot at?" Babcock asked.

"The man who followed him." Shevlin nodded to indicate Hollister, whose boots were still muddy. "Whoever it was thought I'd caught him, and he took a blast at me."

"Nobody followed me!" Hollister exclaimed sharply. "They don't even know I'm in this part of the country!"

"Gentry knew," Babcock reminded him.

"Gib's all right. He's cattle."

"Is he?" Babcock asked skeptically. "You'd better be almighty sure."

Hollister was on edge and belligerent. He had always been a fool, trying to spend with the spenders, gamble with the sharpers, test his strength with the strongest. Sooner or later he would get himself killed, and others with him. Mike Shevlin wanted nothing between himself and Hollister but distance.

"I hear Gentry killed Eli Patterson?" Mike said it like a question.

The atmosphere of the loft altered in some subtle fashion. With years of violence and tension behind him, Mike knew when he had touched a nerve, and he had now.

"Never did figure that out." Babcock was honestly puzzled. "It wasn't like Eli to carry a gun."

"Whoever says he carried a gun," Shevlin replied shortly, "lies. Eli was a Quaker, and he lived by it."

"You can't be sure of that," Hollister protested.

"I knew him."

"The hell with that! You never know a man until he's pushed.

All right, you came here to sleep, so sleep. We don't want any argument."

Shevlin walked to a pile of straw, pulled some out and scattered more over it, then lay down with his slicker stretched over him.

As he relaxed he thought of Eli Patterson. Patterson had lived by his code, and so must Shevlin live by his, different though they might be. In the last analysis it was all a man had to live by. Patterson, a man of peace, had died by the gun. It remained to be seen how Shevlin would die. This was what he was thinking as his eyes closed. And this was in his mind when he awakened to broad daylight and an empty loft.

He climbed down the ladder and stirred the few coals into a fire. Someone had been considerate enough to leave the coffee-pot among the coals. The coffee was hot as hell itself, and black as sin.

Well, now that he was here, what was he to do? What could he do but what he had always done? He would bull his way in, worry the ones who had something to cover up, and force them into some kind of a move. When men moved hastily they often made mistakes. . . .

He would start with Mason. He saddled up and rode into town.

When he stabled his horse at the livery stable he ignored the hostler who sat tipped back in a cane-bottomed chair chewing the stem of an ancient pipe. He was a thin old man with a narrow face and shrewd blue eyes that told nothing.

Shevlin walked to the door of the stable and stood there, lighting a Spanish cigar. As his hands cupped around the match, he spoke without turning his head. "You're a long way from home, Brazos."

"This here's home, an' don't you be a-spoilin' it for me!"

"All I want is information."

"In this town? That's the last thing you'll get. This here town is scared. Ever'body rollin' in money, an' ever'body scared."

"Have you heard the name of Jack Moorman?" Shevlin asked.

"That's one of the things scares 'em. Seems he was beat to death in the street one night, but nobody seen it, an' nobody believes it."

"Any talk about it?"

"Not no more. On'y once in a while somebody gets liquored up. Seems ever'body in Rafter suddenly set out to get rich, an' the on'y two honest men in town got stiff-necked about it. Moorman was one of 'em, so he got himself killed . . . handy-like."

"Clagg?"

"Her husband is Dr. Rupert Clagg, a physician and surgeon."

"Related to Clagg Merriam?"

"A second cousin, I believe. It was Mr. Merriam who influenced them to come to Rafter, I think."

Mike Shevlin combed his hair as he looked in the mirror. He knew too little of what was going on here. He felt that he was like a blind man in a strange room filled with objects unfamiliar to him, whose design had no meaning for him.

Clagg Merriam had been a silent partner of Eli Patterson's, but he had his hand in half a dozen enterprises. He had owned this hotel, and probably still did. He speculated in cattle, too.

Shevlin remembered him now, a tall, too handsome man who dressed well and never seemed to do anything, yet actually did a great deal.

"If you're that cautious," he said to the girl, "you must have a reason."

The green eyes looked directly into his. "I will be honest with you, Mr. Shevlin. I sent a man here to investigate. He was killed. They said it was an accident. He had gone to work in the mine and somebody dropped some drill steel down a manway when he was coming up the ladder."

That was an ugly way to die. In the narrow limits of the manway there was no chance of escape from falling drills—and small chance of accident, when it came to that. His miner's lamp would have been clearly visible, and one was supposed to call "Timber!" before dropping anything. Or at least that had been the rule in hard-rock mines where Mike had worked.

"Why would they want to kill him?" he asked.

She opened her bag and removed an object wrapped in a handkerchief. She unfolded the handkerchief and placed a chunk of ore in his hand.

It was heavy, and it was literally cobwebbed with gold. High-grade . . . high-grade ore. "If there's much of that, you're making a mint," he said.

"That is just the point, Mr. Shevlin. The mine barely pays for itself. There are some months when it does not even do that. That piece of ore came to me in a package with no return address and no comment. It was then I sent the man to investigate."

She hesitated. "Mr. Shevlin, when I was growing up I lived in California and Nevada, where there were mining towns and cattle towns, and in coming here I passed through several such towns. I do not believe I have ever seen a town so prosperous as this one."

"What is it you want me to do?"

"I believe a rich strike has been made, and that my gold is being high-graded . . . stolen. I want you to find out if this is true; and if it is, who is buying the gold, and where it is kept. Then"—she lifted her eyes to his—"I want you to stop the high-grading and recover the gold."

He gave her an incredulous smile. "I don't know what Brazos told you, Miss Tennison, but I don't believe any one man could do what you ask."

"You can do it."

He crossed to the window and looked down at the town. Until she mentioned the town's prosperity, he had not given it a thought. His mind had been too preoccupied with his own weariness when he arrived, and with the problem of Eli Patterson; yet some subtle atmosphere about the town had worried him, and now he knew what it was.

Brazos had phrased it perfectly: everybody rolling in money, and everybody scared.

But how did you fight corruption when all were corrupt?

Turning back from the window, he asked, "You said somebody wanted to buy the mine?"

"The first offer came from Hollister and Evans. That was quite a while ago. I refused to sell. The second came a few months later from a man named Mason. He wished, he said, to close down the mine and reactivate the Rafter H cattle company.

"The Mason offer was repeated a short time ago, but the letter was from the Rafter Mining Company, saying their man Mason had made a previous offer. It was simply repeated in the same terms."

"Who signed that letter?"

"A man named Ben Stowe."

Ben Stowe!

The last time Shevlin had seen Stowe he was living in an abandoned homesteader's shack, rustling a few head of cattle, and riding with a wild bunch. And now he was offering to buy a mine!

"What you say about the town," he said softly, "is true—it is prosperous. My guess would be that everybody connected with the mine is high-grading, if the stuff is actually there, and every place of business in town is taking gold in trade, or buying it. As to recovering your gold, I'd say it would be impossible. By now it must be lost in the normal channels of trade."

"I do not think so."

She leaned forward, her hands in her lap. "Mr. Shevlin, I

believe all that gold is right here in Rafter. I believe someone
with capital—perhaps the people who wish to buy the mine—
are buying the gold from the stores and holding it. I believe
they intend to buy the mine with my gold, then dispose of the
remainder after they own the property."

She got to her feet. "Mr. Shevlin, gold is not easy to conceal;
and as you undoubtedly know, the gold from no two mines is
exactly the same. It is difficult to dispose of gold without it
being known, and no sales have been reported from this area,
no gold has appeared that cannot be accounted for.

"You think I am only a foolish girl, but believe me, Mr.
Shevlin, my grandfather treated me like a son in many respects,
and among other things he taught me a great deal about
business, and a great deal about gold and the marketing of
gold.

"The Pinkertons checked on gold sales for me, beyond what
I could do through the normal channels of exchange. I do not
believe the Pinkertons could find out what is happening here. I
believe it will take somebody with local knowledge."

He glanced at her with respect. This was a girl who knew
her own mind, and was uncommonly shrewd along with it.

High-grading, the stealing of rich ore from a mine or smelter,
was always difficult to control. Opening a change room where
the miners changed from their digging clothes to their outside
clothes could stop some of it, and checking lunchboxes or
canteens could, too, but where there was high-grade ore there
would always be ways to steal it.

If what she believed was true, the men who controlled the
working of the mine must have deliberately permitted the
miners their chance to high-grade in order to involve them,
and the community itself, in the crime of high-grading. Then
the operators of the mine simply kept the vastly greater amount
of gold for themselves, allowing only a small amount to go
through legitimate channels, and this small amount was bought
from the storekeepers to keep it out of circulation.

It required capital, rigid control, and some shrewd operation
to make it work. Once the mine was owned by the operators of
the high-grade ring, then they might take other steps; certainly
they must realize such an operation could not long continue.

"I will pay, Mr. Shevlin," the girl went on. "I will pay well. I
will give you ten per cent of all you recover, and if my calcula-
tions are near the truth the recovery might reach a half a
million dollars."

"You'd have to trust me. What's to keep me from locating
the gold and keeping it for myself?"

She smiled at him. "Mr. Shevlin, you have a very bad reputation. You are said to have stolen cattle, it is said that you are a gunfighter, that you have engaged in public brawls, that you were once friendly with the very men who are robbing me. I have heard all that. Nevertheless, I believe in you."

She gathered her skirts and stepped to the door. "You see, Mr. Shevlin, Brazos was not the only man who told me you could be trusted. Long ago my uncle told my grandfather, when I was present, that there was one man in Rafter who could be trusted under any circumstances. He said that no matter what anybody said, Mike Shevlin was an honorable man, and an honest man."

Now who the hell would say a thing like that about him? Turning away, he walked to the window again to keep her from seeing how much her words had touched him.

"Your uncle can't have known me very well," he said.

"He thought he did, Mr. Shevlin, and he believed in you. I think you knew him very well, Mr. Shevlin. His name was Eli Patterson."

THREE

The storm had broken. Scattered clouds raced across the sky, and between them the stars shone like the lights of far-off towns.

He stood alone on the wet street, with enemies all about him. It was after midnight, and only a few lights looked out upon the rain-darkened walks, the muddy streets, and the blank faces of the false-fronted stores across the way.

Now, at night, it might have been any little western town, but it was not just any town. It was a town built on deceit and theft, a town corrupted by its own greed, a town that had arrived at this point without realizing how deep were the depths into which it descended.

Mike Shevlin looked gloomily from under the black brim of his hat. He looked upon the town with no hatred. Here his best friend had been killed, brutally shot down in an alley because he had the courage to stand against evil. But Mike Shevlin knew all too well how easy it was to accept that first dishonest dollar, and he knew all the excuses a man could give himself.

After all, a man would say, the gold comes out of the ground, why shouldn't I get some of it? Everybody else is getting it, why shouldn't I? There were a multitude of easy excuses, useful in all such cases; but the trouble was that evil can plant a seed, and the seed can grow. From easy acceptance of a minor misdemeanor, one can come to acceptance of a minor crime, and from a minor crime to a major one. And this town had now accepted robbery on a large scale . . . perhaps larger than any one man knew, except for the leaders. And they had accepted murder.

Thereby came fear. For murder breeds murder, and those

who have killed once for gain, will kill again; and those who have agreed to ignore a murder, will ignore another if it is to protect some small security of their own—property, or guilt they themselves possess.

Mike Shevlin knew this because there had been a time when he had himself been guilty. It had seemed a great lark to run off a few steers to sell for a spree in town. And then suddenly he had wondered how he would feel if those had been his father's cattle, or his own.

There comes a time for a man to draw a line, and Mike Shevlin had drawn his, and he had ridden away from Rafter, from Gib Gentry, Ben Stowe, and all the rest of them. And now he had come back to a changed town. The old, easy friendship was gone. The hospitality of the West was no longer here. This town was alive with fear, with suspicion, and with hatred, and he, of all people, would find no welcome.

For surely every man here, and every woman too, was his enemy. What he had been asked to do and what he wished to do were bound together. If he found the man who had killed Eli Patterson, he would also expose the plot to high-grade gold; and if he did that the prosperity of this town would end.

What was right, and what was just? Had he the right to come into this place and shatter its prosperity? Here people dressed better, lived better, had better houses than in other such towns. There was more money spent over the bars, more money in the stores; but with the prosperity there would be, for some men, a sense of power. The leaders of all this, the men who created and planned it, had won acceptance of corruption, and now there was no limit to what they might ask and force the town to accept—or was there?

There must be people here, good people, restless with what was happening, people who wanted to be free of fear. But he did not know these people, and had he known them he knew they would not trust him, not Mike Shevlin. What he did he must do alone. And now he stood there pondering on it.

Across the street and down a few doors, a man stepped out to the edge of the walk and looked across at Shevlin. Mike knew that look, that attitude. The man was suspicious.

To be a stranger in this town, an unaccounted-for stranger, was enough to excite fear. Mike Shevlin's every instinct warned him he was in danger, danger increasing with every minute. These people had been parties to theft and had turned their eyes from murder . . . and they would turn their eyes from another.

There were too many pairs of new boots, too many expensive

saddles here; too many men had ivory- or pearl-handled guns. Somebody had been shrewd enough to let a whole community get its fingers sticky. By simply looking the other way while the miners high-graded a little gold, the men who operated the mines had made the townspeople accomplices to their own theft.

Each buyer of high-grade, each tradesman who accepted it over a counter, took a portion of profit from the transaction, and because it was known by all to be stolen gold, they took a higher profit than usual.

Eli Patterson and Jack Moorman were dead, and they were men Mike Shevlin had respected. Each in his way had been kind to the lonely, half-starved boy who rode his crow-bait of a horse into town. Each in his own way had helped to make him a better man than he had any right to be. . . . Some things Mike Shevlin had told no man.

It was true he had worked with his uncle on a mining claim, but it was a miserable claim that made them a living, no more. And then there had come the day when the roof caved in, burying his uncle under the mountain.

The boy who was Mike Shevlin had walked away, leading his horse down the mountain because it was in bad shape to carry him over the rough terrain. The mine tunnel was a fitting grave for his uncle, and he lay buried there with the hopes he had never quite lost.

Of his father, Mike had never talked. He had been killed out on the plains by men who found him selling whiskey to Indians. His mother had died a few years later in a miserable shack on the edge of town, a faraway cow town. But she had taught him a few things: to make his own way in the world; to accept nothing he had not earned.

That had been little enough on which to build a life until, after leaving his uncle's claim, he had come to Rafter and met Eli Patterson, and afterwards Jack Moorman. Instinctively he honored these men who stood staunchly by what they believed. The thought of these men was in his mind now.

The Bon Ton Restaurant, just down the street, was still open. Mike crossed over and went down the walk. Opening the door of the restaurant, he stepped inside.

The coal-oil lamps with reflectors behind them filled the room with light. There were several unoccupied small tables, and two long tables covered with white cloths, for family-style meals. A sideboard covered with glasses and stacks of plates stood against the wall; on its right a door opened to the kitchen.

Three men, apparently miners off shift, sat together at the end of the nearest table. At the far end of the other table sat two men, one in the rough clothes of the frontier, the other in a well-tailored dark gray suit.

Shevlin dropped to a seat on the bench at the nearest table, admiring the smooth expanse of white linen. The last time he had eaten in this restaurant the tables were covered with oilcloth.

The waitress brought him coffee, and over it he began to consider the situation. He must talk to Mason. He felt a curious reluctance to meet Gentry . . . after all, the man had been his comrade, they had worked and fought side by side. Now he thought that Gentry might become his enemy, and he did not want that.

But Gentry must be protecting somebody. If he had not killed Eli himself—and Brazos's evidence implied he had not—he knew who had killed him.

But why should Gentry go out on a limb to protect someone else? Who was that important to him? It was unlike Gentry to take credit for another man's killing . . . especially the killing of Eli Patterson.

As Mike Shevlin drank his coffee, he looked at the two men at the other table. The man in the tailored suit looked familiar, but Mike's attention was diverted by one of the miners at his own table. He was a stocky, red-headed man, who had been staring hard at Mike, trying to attract his eyes.

"You've come to the wrong town," the miner said suddenly; "we ran all the cattlemen out of here long ago."

Mike Shevlin smiled pleasantly. "I'm double-action—cattle or mines. I can swing a single-jack or double-jack as good as the next man."

"Where'd you ever work in the mines?"

"All over the country. Silverton, Colorado . . . down in the Cerbat Range in Arizona . . . over at Pioche and Frisco."

"They're full up here. Nobody hirin'."

"Doesn't look like I'll find a job, then, does it?" The redhead was trouble-hunting. The type and the pattern were familiar. There was one in every town, always trying to prove how tough he was . . . sometimes there was more than one. And they were rarely the really hard cases. They had nothing to prove.

Deliberately, Mike kept his tone mild. He understood the pattern and accepted it, but if Red wanted to push trouble he must do it on his own. He would get no trouble from Shevlin. There was trouble enough without that.

At the other table the man in frontier clothes looked around. "If you're a miner, I can use you," he said. "I'm Burt Parry—I've got a claim in Cottonwood Canyon. If you're serious about a job, meet me at six-thirty for breakfast here, and we'll ride out."

Parry got up from the table. "I'll have those figures for you, Mr. Merriam," he said to the man in the gray suit. "I'll have them tomorrow or the day after."

He paused by Shevlin's table. "Tomorrow morning, six-thirty . . . right?"

"I'll see you," Shevlin said. "I'll be here."

The waitress placed a dish of food before him, and he picked up his knife and fork. Merriam, the man had said. That would be Clagg Merriam. Mike had seen him only once or twice in the old days, for Merriam was often out of town. He was a bigger man than Mike remembered, with a strong face and a smile on his lips that did not reach to his eyes.

The redhead moved down the table opposite Shevlin. "You didn't tell him your name," he said.

"He didn't ask," Shevlin replied mildly.

"Well, I'm asking."

"None of your damn' business." Shevlin spoke in such a gentle voice that it was a moment before the meaning got to the redhead.

When he realized what had been said, Red smiled. He wiped his palms on the front of his shirt. Then he stood up very slowly, still smiling, and reached across the table to grasp the front of Shevlin's shirt.

Shevlin dropped his knife and fork, and his left hand grasped Red's wrist, jerking him forward. There was an empty dish on the table that had held mutton. With his right hand Shevlin pushed the miner's face down into the dish and, gripping Red's left hand, he coolly wiped his face around in the cold mutton grease.

Abruptly, Shevlin let go and Red came up, half over the table and spluttering with fury. Shevlin jerked the butt of his palm up under the man's chin and sent him toppling back over the bench to the floor beyond. During the entire action he had scarcely risen from his seat.

For a second, Red lay stunned, then with an oath he started to rise. A voice stopped him.

"Cut it out, Red! This time you've swung too wide a loop. This gent would clobber you good!"

Shevlin looked around. There he was—older, of course, and heavier. Yes, and better dressed than Shevlin ever remembered him. His face was puffy, and he looked like a man who was living too well—something nobody could have said of the old Gentry.

"Hello, Gib," Mike said. "It's been a while."

Gentry thrust out a big hand. "Mike! Mike Shevlin!" There was no mistaking the pleasure in Gentry's voice. "Man, am I glad to see you!"

Shevlin took the hand. It was all wrong, he thought. Whatever else Gentry might do, he would not kill a man like Eli. A tough man, Gentry was, even a cruel one at times, but a man who fought with fighting men.

Shevlin was aware of the room's attention. Clagg Merriam was watching them, his face unreadable. Red was slowly wiping the grease from his face.

"Come down the street, Mike," Gentry was saying, "and I'll buy you a drink for old time's sake."

Reluctantly, Shevlin got up from the table. The last thing he wanted was a drink. What he wanted was food and coffee, gallons of coffee.

"The town's changed," Shevlin said tentatively as they emerged on the street. "I don't see many of the old faces."

"Gone . . . gone with the cattle business."

Shevlin waited until they had taken a few strides, and then he asked, "What happened to Ray Hollister?"

Gentry's smile vanished. "Ray? Got too big for his boots, Ray did. He left the country . . . and just in time."

"He always did try to take big steps."

"Say!" There was obvious relief in Gentry's tone. "I'd forgotten about the time you two tangled out at Rock Springs. You never did get along with him."

The thought seemed to please him. Gentry rested a big hand on Shevlin's shoulder as they reached the door of the Gold Miner's Daughter. Mike restrained his distaste. He had never liked to be touched, and had not cared for Gentry's backslapping good humor.

To get to the point, he asked, "Are you ranching, Gib?"

"Me?" Gentry opened the door, and went on speaking as they entered. "The cattle business is a thing of the past in this country. No, I'm in the freighting business. Hauling for the mines—supplies in, gold out, working twenty to thirty rigs all the time."

Mike saw no familiar faces in the saloon. Gentry lifted a hand and the bartender tossed him a bottle, which Gib caught deftly. Then the bartender tossed two shot glasses, which Gentry caught just as easily with the other hand. He had always been fast with his hands for a big man . . . and fast with a gun.

Gentry was in a genial, talkative mood, and Shevlin was willing to listen. A cowhand, Gentry told him, had struck gold on the old Rafter H while sinking a post hole. Without saying a word to anyone he had gone off to San Francisco and obtained financial backing, then returned and bought the Rafter H headquarters area.

Polluted water from the mill flowed into the creek, spelling ruin for the Rafter H and the other cattle outfits. They fought, and among the casualties was the cowhand who had discovered the gold.

"Mighty convenient, I figure," Gentry commented, refilling his glass, "but it didn't do anybody any good. Turned out he had sold his entire interest to that Frisco outfit. There was trouble a-plenty with Turkeytrack and Rafter, but nothing we couldn't manage."

"We?"

Gentry winked. "Now, Mike, you know ol' Gib. I never let any grass grow under my feet, you know that, an' there's more money in gold than in cattle. The trouble started when I hired on as guard at the Sun Strike."

"Trouble?"

"Shooting trouble, Mike. Ben Stowe was boss of the guards, an' you know Ben. He knew where to pick up a few salty boys down in the Panhandle country, and after we'd buried two or three of the local boys that was the end of it."

Trust Ben Stowe to know who had to be killed. The backbone of any cow outfit lies in two or three fighting men whom the rest follow. Put them out of the picture, and the rest would be likely to lose heart. Mike Shevlin had seen it managed that way more than once, and had seen it tried at other times.

"Gib, who is the law around here?"

"You on the dodge?"

"Who is he?"

"Aw, you've nothing to worry about. You know how it is with the law in these western towns. The law is always local law, so busy skinning its own cats it hasn't time to worry about anybody who doesn't make trouble. You could shoot half a dozen men in Denver or Cheyenne, and nobody would bother you anywhere else as long as you stayed out of trouble. . . . But the law here is Wilson Hoyt."

Wilson Hoyt, of all people! He was a burly bear of a man,

broad and thick and muscular, but fast enough to have killed a man who had the drop on him. He was credited with seventeen killings, all on the side of the law. Of all the men who might be in this town, the one most likely to know about Mike Shevlin was Hoyt.

Hollister, Gentry, and Mason only knew the boy who had ridden away, and ten years and more can deepen and widen a man, they can salt him down with toughness and wisdom. And Mike had been gone thirteen years. Of them all, Hoyt would understand him more than the others, and Hoyt had seen him looking at Eli's grave and would know why he had come back.

Gentry rambled on, taking a third drink while Mike was nursing his first. He talked about the good old days, and it came over Mike that Gentry still thought of him as a friend.

"You got to hand it to Ray," Gentry said confidentially. "He always wanted to be a big man, and when gold was discovered he grabbed at the chance.

"He never came out in the open with it, and the cattle crowd never knew he'd thrown in with the other side. When trouble started—and I always figured his loud mouth caused it—Ray got in touch with the Frisco people and offered to handle negotiations with the ranchers. He and that shyster Evans called themselves a law firm, but you know Ben. When Hollister brought Ben into it he put a rope on trouble.

"When a few of the miners started high-grading a little here and there, Ben argued Ray into looking the other way. But Ben, he said nothing to Ray about the setup he arranged for buying up the gold to keep it out of circulation."

"Where did Ben get that kind of money?"

Gentry gave Mike another wink. "Now, that there is Ben's own secret, but don't you low-rate Ben. Buying up the high-grade kept the news from getting out that Sun Strike was big. They reported low averages from the mine, and nobody knew any different."

By this time Gentry was working on his fourth drink.

"Smart—that was smart thinking," Mike remarked.

"You're not just a-woofing," Gentry said.

Trust Eli not to go along with that, or Jack Moorman for that matter, for Jack had money invested in town business, and he owned Turkeytrack as well. So they had been killed.

Had Ben Stowe realized that Eli Patterson was connected with the San Francisco owners? Shevlin's guess was they had not known. Shevlin had known Eli better than any of them had, and he had never heard him make any reference to relatives or friends in San Francisco . . . or anywhere else, for that matter. Eli had come west from Illinois, and when he talked it was about life back there.

Mike was scarcely listening to Gentry now, and Gib had gone back to talking of the old days, reliving the rough, tough old days of branding, roundups, and cattle drives.

"Remember the time a rattler scared that line-back dun of yours? He went right over the rim an' I'll be damned if you didn't stay with him all the way to the river! If anybody had told me a man could ride a horse down that slope I'd have said he was loco."

Gentry was drunk . . . it was possible that by morning he would have no memory of what he had told Shevlin, and Mike was sure that only the liquor—he had already had a few when they met—had made him talk as freely as he had. That—and something else Mike suddenly realized: Gib Gentry was lonesome.

There was one other fact to consider. Gentry was in the freighting business, and when gold was moved he would do the moving, and there would be nobody to ask questions.

If Ben Stowe had done the planning for this operation he had planned very shrewdly indeed. All the loose ends were nicely tucked in, and everything was under control—everything but Gib Gentry's tongue when he'd had a few drinks. Did they know that?

"What's Burt Parry like?" Mike asked.

"Aw, he's all right. He's got him a two-by-four claim over in the canyon. There's nothing over there, but he sure ain't willing to believe it."

Shevlin pushed back his chair and got up. "I'd better get some sleep." For a moment he rested a hand on Gentry's shoulder. "Good to see you, boy. You watch your step now."

"See you." Gentry seemed about to say something more, but he only added, "So long, kid."

At six o'clock the next morning the man operating Eli's old store was out sweeping the boardwalk. Mike Shevlin strolled inside and the man followed. Shevlin bought what digging clothes he would need, some candles, and a cap-lamp, and then said, "And four boxes of .44's."

The storekeeper glanced up. "You expecting trouble?"

"Man of peace, myself. Figured I'd be off up that canyon workin' for Burt Parry and I'd have me some target practice. I never could hit the broad side of a barn."

Burt Parry was waiting in front of the Nevada House when

Shevlin returned with his packages. "Lady waiting for you," he said, "in the dining room. I heard her asking for you."

He went inside and passed under the arch into the dining room. It was Eve, and she was alone.

"You wanted to see me?"

"I want to offer you a job. At the Three Sevens."

"I heard the cow business was in a bad way around here."

Lowering her voice, she said, "Mr. Shevlin, we need men like you, and whatever else you are, you're cattle."

He felt irritation mounting within him. "All right, you tell me. What kind of a man am I?"

"You've used a gun, and we need guns."

He felt a vast impatience. "Lady, with all due respect, you're talking nonsense." He jerked his head to indicate the Sun Strike and the steady pound of its compressor. "Do you think guns will stop *that*? As long as there's ore in the ground, they'll be there."

"That's not true. If Ray Hollister had been leading us, he would have run Ben Stowe out of the country!"

Shevlin looked at her ironically. "You really believe that? As a fighting man, Ray Hollister couldn't come up to Ben Stowe's boot-tops."

Her anger flared. "If you believe that, there's no job for you at Three Sevens!"

"Sorry . . . but I already have a job. As a miner."

Abruptly, she got to her feet. "Jess Winkler said you were one of them, but I just couldn't believe it. You're just a thief, a common thief!"

She walked out, heels clicking, and he followed to join Burt Parry outside. "Sorry to keep you waiting," he said.

Parry glanced at him. "The lady was in a hurry," he commented.

"When I told her I had a mining job, she called me a thief."

"If you worked for anybody but me," Parry said wryly, "that might be true." He looked straight at Shevlin. "What would you say if I told you some of the ore from the Sun Strike assayed as high as twenty thousand dollars a ton?"

"I'd tell you there was a gent down in Chile found a nugget that weighed four hundred pounds. What I mean is, it could happen once."

"My friend," Parry said seriously, "some of the richest ore I've ever seen came out of that mine, and not just a little bit."

High-grade . . . every miner knew what that meant. Ore so rich a man could carry a month's wages out in his pockets, and two months' wages in a canteen or a lunchbox. He had known of mines where the foreman was paid by miners for the privilege of working. Change rooms could only curb high-grading; they couldn't stop it.

"And nobody talks?" Shevlin asked.

"They're all in it. I'm not, but I don't have much to say, and I don't try to leave town. Sometimes I wonder if I *could* leave. Maybe I'm alive only because I haven't tried."

"You're taking a chance even telling me. How do you know I'm not their spy?"

"You couldn't be. You're in trouble, Shevlin."

"*I* am?"

"Don't expect reason from any of them, Mike. They're in too deep, and all of them are running scared. I was advised not to hire you."

"Why me?"

"There was a man named Hollister—and there's the fact that you arrived just at this time. They are deathly afraid of Hollister, Mike, and if they locate him, he's a dead man."

"You know a lot."

"I wish I knew less. I have a friend or two, and they tell me things." Parry looked at Mike's gun. "Are you any good with that?"

"I get along."

Parry started toward the livery stable and Mike walked along with him. He could feel eyes on them, eyes watching them down the street. Suddenly he realized that he could have done nothing worse than go to work for Burt Parry, the one man who was an outsider.

No matter. He was in up to his ears, anyway, and he had a hunch that if he got out he would get out shooting. For the first time in years he was suddenly conscious of the gun at his hip.

FOUR

In his office above the bank, Ben Stowe tipped back in his big leather chair and stared thoughtfully out the window toward the trees along the creek. He had come far since the morning fourteen years ago when Jack Moorman fired him off the Turkeytrack.

He had never forgotten that day. Old Jack had been seated in his hide chair with a shotgun across his knees when he told Ben Stowe he was a cow thief, and probably a murderer as well, and also told him what would happen if he was ever found on Turkeytrack range again.

Ben Stowe, big, powerful, and tough, had stood there and taken it, but even now he flushed at the memory, grudgingly admitting to himself that he had been afraid. In all his life he had feared no man but Jack Moorman. Dead now for several years, Jack Moorman still had the power to destroy him.

Until the discovery of gold on Rafter, Ben Stowe had been merely another rustler. Not that anybody else in the Rafter country had dared accuse him, but it was generally known.

The gold discovery had been his big chance, and he jumped to take it. From the first he had understood the possibilities . . . some of them. The idea of seizing the mine itself he owed to Ray Hollister.

Hollister had recognized the power that lay in control of the mines, and he grabbed for it. But in this he overestimated himself and underestimated others. He had looked upon Ben Stowe as a down-at-heel hired man, and he forgot to consider that the fires of ambition might burn just as strongly in another as in himself. And suddenly Ray was out and Ben was in control.

The end was near. The offers had been made, not only for

the Sun Strike, but for the Glory Hole as well, offers large
enough to interest them as an escape from a constant drain, yet
not large enough to cause them to wonder.

Ben Stowe stared at the trees and thought of the years
ahead. Once the mine was in the possession of himself and his
partner, he would cut all his ties with the old life, and cut them
with a ruthless hand. The mine would make millions; business
in the town would be worked back to normal, not so suddenly
as to cause trouble, but with a deft hand. People would soon
forget what Ben Stowe had done, or remember it, as the West
often did, as the harmless escapades of another time.

The door from the outer office opened and Ben Stowe felt a
swift surge of anger. He was beginning not to like it when
someone presumed enough to come bursting into his office.
But this was Gib Gentry.

Suddenly he saw Gentry with new eyes. Gentry and he were
old friends, but in the future that Stowe planned, where would
Gentry fit? And with sudden, chill awareness he knew he
would not fit at all.

Gentry dropped into a chair and put his boots on Ben's desk,
and Ben Stowe again felt that swift anger. Gib was too damned
familiar. But even as he thought that, he was surprised at
himself.

Why the sudden fury? He had always been a man who kept
his temper on a leash. It was that coldness and control that had
brought him to where he was . . . why the sudden anger now?

Gentry bit the end from a cigar. "Hell, Ben, you should've
been down the street. Who the hell do you think I ran into?"

"Mike Shevlin?"

"Now how the hell did you know that?"

Ben Stowe was pleased with himself. It was a little thing, a
simple thing, but long ago he had realized the importance of
knowing what was going on around the country, and had taken
pains to see that he learned of new arrivals, or of any occur-
rence that was out of the ordinary. He had several sources of
information, one of which was the marshal.

As a member of the town council, he had directed the
marshal in his duties. All he had learned now was that a
stranger, a very salty customer, had been up on Boot Hill
looking at Eli's grave, but when he put that together with a few
other items he could make a fairly safe guess.

Gentry pushed his hat back on his head. "Damn it, Ben!
Seemed like old times, havin' Mike around. He looks good,
too."

Ben Stowe shuffled some papers on his desk and wished

Gentry would go. Gib had always been a bit of a damned fool. Always ready to pick up a fast dollar, but carrying a wide streak of sentiment. After all, he and Shevlin had never been all that thick.

"Look, Gib, you be careful what you say. There was a meeting at the old mill last night . . . and then another man rode up through the rain. My man thought it was either Hollister or somebody following him. Whoever it was put a bullet in my man."

"You can forget that. Mike never had a damn' bit of use for Ray, and vice versa. Ray's small change, and Mike always knew it."

"I never cottoned to him, anyway," Ben said irritably. "I know he was a friend of yours, but what does it look like, him riding in just at this time? You know how tight everything is. If we have trouble now it could blow the lid off—or tighten it up so hard it might be years before we could make it pay off."

"Hollister's just a sorehead. He can't hurt us."

Ben Stowe gave him an impatient look. "Gib, you never could see past your nose. There's one thing you forget—Ray Hollister could go to the governor."

Gentry was incredulous. "The *governor*? Aw, Ben, you're lettin' this get on your nerves! What interest would the governor have in this place?"

"The governor," Ben Stowe replied, "married Jack Moorman's daughter, that's all. And if that isn't enough, the governor's father rode in here on a cattle drive as a partner of Jack's, and after his father died, Jack practically raised him. He was in Washington when old Jack was killed, and if he had been governor then, he'd have raised hell."

Gentry shifted uneasily in his chair. All the pleased excitement of Shevlin's return was gone. He took his feet down from the desk and wished he had never come to see Ben. Things just weren't the same any more. Ben was impatient all the time; he never took time for a drink with him, never talked it up like in the old days. And now this about the governor. Of course, he remembered it, now that he thought of it. He had forgotten, that was all. Anyway, Jack Moorman had been dead for years—that was all over.

"Hollister couldn't prove anything," he said. "He wasn't even there."

"There are some who were," Stowe replied sourly, "and when a horse starts swishin' his tail there's no telling what burrs he'll pick up."

Gentry was suddenly hot and uncomfortable. He had never

forgotten the contempt in old Jack's eyes as they battered him to his knees. That look had penetrated to the very core of Gentry's being, and for months he had waked up shaking with fright and bathed in sweat, remembering those eyes.

The old man never had a chance. Struck down from behind, his gun belt had been cut through, removing any chance of resistance. They had not wanted to use a gun or a knife. There was bad feeling between the miners and the cattlemen, and it was pay day night. They planned for it to look like something done by drunken miners.

"If you think so much of Shevlin," Stowe was saying, "you get him out of here. He could make trouble."

When the door closed after Gentry, Stowe put his feet on his desk. No need to tell Gentry the word on Shevlin was already out. There was no longer any need to tell Gentry anything. After they moved the gold, something would have to be done about Gib Gentry. He had outlived his usefulness.

Gentry stood outside under the awning staring down the street. He bit the end from a fresh cigar. The hell with Ben Stowe. The hell with them all.

He had had more to drink than he had ever had before, but what did it mean, after all? He never had any fun any more, and Stowe had changed. Hardly talked to him any more, and whenever Gentry came around Ben made it seem as if he was talking nonsense, or was acting like a fool.

Gib Gentry stood there on the street and looked bleakly into a future that held no promise. He wasn't a kid any more. And he was hitting the bottle too hard. He had known that for some time, but he had never actually allowed it to shape into words before. Uneasily, his thoughts kept returning to Ben Stowe. Ben was a hard man. He had best step very lightly.

Suddenly he was swept by anger. Step lightly? Who the hell did Ben think he was, anyway? Why the hell should he step lightly for Ben Stowe or any other man?

Now Ben had told him to get Mike Shevlin out of town. Just how was he to go about *that?* It had been a long time since Gib had seen Mike or heard more than vague rumors of him, but any man with half an eye could see Mike Shevlin had been riding where the owl hooted and the long winds blew . . . no mistake about that.

It was a hell of a situation when a man like Shevlin might be killed—and he would take a lot of killing. Ben Stowe could be almighty dumb sometimes. He should be able to see that the best thing he could do would be to leave Mike Shevlin alone.

Gib Gentry had always considered himself a hard, dangerous man, and he had been all of that, but he was also a man with a love for reliving the old days, sharing a bottle, and talking of the old times. The truth was that Gib, like many another, had never quite grown up. In reliving the old days and replaying the old games, he avoided a hard look at whatever future might lie ahead of him.

It was going to rain again; clouds were gathering over the mountains. Gentry's cigar had gone out. He stared at it, disgusted, and then turned and walked down the street. Yes, Ben had changed. He cared damned little for his old friends. Somewhere in the back of Gib's brain a tiny bell sounded its warning, but Gib did not hear it. He was thinking about a drink.

Mike Shevlin followed Burt Parry up the narrow canyon, between occasional trees, clumps of brush, and tumbled boulders or slides of broken rock. When they reached the claim Parry said, "There's good water at a spring about sixty yards up the canyon, and unless you fancy yourself as a cook, I'll put the grub together."

"By the time I'd eaten my own cooking the second time, I decided against that."

He stripped the saddle from his horse, and glanced around, but there was little enough to see. Parry's claim shanty stood on the bench made by the mine's dump. It was a simple two-room cabin, hastily but securely put together. About thirty feet from it was a small corral, on one side of which was a lean-to shack used as a tool house. Beyond was the opening of the tunnel.

Up the canyon, just visible from where they stood, there was another dump, larger than their own. No buildings were visible there.

"Whose claim is that?" Shevlin asked.

"It's abandoned. That was the discovery claim for Sun Strike. The gold was found on the mesa right above there, so they decided to drift into the hill from here, but they gave up when they found the ore body lay on the other side of the hill."

When they sat down to eat, darkness was filling the canyon, softening all the harshness of the bleak hills. Shevlin, drinking his second cup of coffee, was listening to the birds in the bottom of the canyon. Suddenly, the sound ceased. Parry was talking, and if he noticed the change he gave no indication of it.

"Many visitors out here?" Shevlin asked.

"The vein seems to be widening out, and I believe in about sixty feet . . . What was that you said?"

"I asked if you had many visitors?"

"Here? Why would anybody come out here? They all think I'm crazy to work this claim. I haven't had two visitors in the past four months."

"How far back does this canyon go?"

Parry shrugged. "How the hell should I know? I never followed it up. About a mile further along it narrows down to just a slash in the mountain. They say you can touch both sides with outstretched arms. Hell of a mess of rock back in there."

Mike Shevlin got up and went to the door. He stood there, leaning against the doorjamb. It might have been a roving lion, but he had a hunch the birds had shut up because a man was passing.

"When you get up in the morning," Parry said, "you can muck out that rock I shot down on my last shift. I'll be riding back into town."

"It's a prosperous town," Shevlin commented.

"Less you say about that the better. I stay away from town most of the time, and I never talk about anything but my own claim, or whatever news we hear from out of town."

At daylight, with Parry gone, Mike Shevlin went into the tunnel and settled down to work. He had always rather liked working with a shovel; it had the advantage of giving a man time to think, and he had a lot of that to do.

What it shaped up to was that Ray Hollister had been using the cattlemen as a wedge to get back into power, a power he had been aced out of . . . and somebody was going to get hurt.

Ben Stowe was no hot-headed, conceited fool like Hollister. He was cold, cruel, and tough in a way Hollister never dreamed of. If Hollister chose to get himself killed, that was his own business, but the way he was headed he would get others killed as well.

Eve believed in Hollister, and it was likely that she was a little in love with him. Babcock was fiercely loyal to Hollister, as he had always been; but had he any idea what Hollister was planning?

The town was rich and suspicious and frightened. It was afraid of losing its riches, it was afraid of being exposed, and yet every one of them probably knew the lid was about to blow off.

Somebody had killed Eli Patterson and Jack Moorman, then had moved in and taken control. Undoubtedly all reports leaving town went from Ben Stowe's office. The shift bosses would be carefully selected henchmen of his. Everyone in town, in one way or another, had a stake in keeping things as they were.

There was, of course, Wilson Hoyt.

If there was one man Shevlin hoped to have on his side it was Hoyt, and so far as he knew, Hoyt was incorruptible. He was a man of simple purpose. His job was to insure peace in the town, and that he intended to do. Hoyt, Shevlin was sure, had no hand in what was going on, although he might be aware of it. He would make no stand unless somehow it affected his work.

While Mike's mind was busy with these thoughts, he kept working with his shovel. Now he wheeled his loaded wheelbarrow to the end of the plank runway and dumped it. As he turned around to go back, he saw Eve Bancroft ride her horse up on the dump.

"You're wasting your time," she said. "There's no high-grade here."

"I was beginning to guess as much." He sensed her dislike, and wondered why she had come.

Her eyes seemed to tighten a little. "Mike, we want you on our side."

He put the wheelbarrow down and straightened up. "You're choosing up sides? What for?" He pushed his hat back and wiped away the sweat with the back of his hand. "You don't think shooting a few miners will stop them, do you?"

She repressed her animosity with difficulty. "When this fight is over this will be cattle country again, and nothing but cattle."

"You can't drive pigs from a trough with a switch."

"Ray thinks different."

"Hollister always tried taking in too much territory, but he's not that much of a fool."

Her fury flared. "Ray Hollister was a big man here before, and he will be again! Now that he's back, things will change!"

"Eve," Shevlin said patiently, "Hollister will get you hurt. He was never a big man anywhere, and never will be. He just can't cut the mustard. Years ago, when you were just a child, Ray Hollister had a good ranch that could have kept him comfortable for the rest of his days, but it wasn't enough for him.

"He wanted to be top dog. He hung around Jack Moorman, and when Jack spat, Ray spat twice as hard; when Moorman grumbled, Ray swore. Well, he tried to be bigger than he was cut out to be, and they ran him out of the country. This time they'll bury him."

"You're jealous! You were always afraid of him!"

"Ask him about the whipping I gave him out at Rock Springs. The truth is, Eve, that nobody was ever afraid of Ray."

She wheeled her horse, her features rigid with anger. "I've tried for the last time! You leave the country, Mike Shevlin, and leave it fast! You've had your chance."

Regretfully, he watched her race her horse down the canyon. She was a pretty young woman, but Ray Hollister had convinced her, and she was one of those who could never see the other side of any question. . . . Ray was not so old, when you came to think of it. He would be about thirty-eight now, and Eve Bancroft was twenty or so. And that much of a spread in ages was not uncommon in the West . . . or in other places, for that matter.

The trouble was that Ray Hollister, driven by a blind fury to realize his ambition, would get somebody killed. All the way along the line Ray had missed the boat, and to a man of his ego that was intolerable. He was striking out frantically now in desperation and bitterness. If he had ever thought of anyone but himself, except those successful people he had formerly idolized, he certainly was thinking of no one else now. Not even of Eve.

As Shevlin worked at the muck pile in the hot end of the drift, sweat pouring from him, it came to him suddenly that there was a way to stop all this. If the richness of the mines could be brought into the open, suddenly exposed, then Ben Stowe and his crowd would have nothing to fight for, and it would stop Ray Hollister too.

The news that the mines were rich would immediately destroy any chance of Stowe or any of his crowd buying the mines. It would bring in a rush of outsiders, and further buying of high-grade would have to be curbed. And the ranchers would realize, no matter what Hollister might say, that the mines were not about to be abandoned.

But how could he, Mike Shevlin, bring that about? Nobody would accept the word of a drifting cowhand with a bad reputation. He must have evidence, concrete evidence in the shape of high-grade ore. Moreover, he must locate the cache where the high-grade was hidden. If he did not do this, the thieves would certainly take the gold and escape when their thefts were disclosed. And in such case, Laine Tennison would be defrauded.

By the time Mike had mucked out the drift it was mid-afternoon. Right at the face it was easier, because Burt Parry had gotten a sheet of boiler plate from someone and had placed it on the floor of the drift before firing his shots and bringing down the muck on top of the sheet. This was old practice in the larger mines, but you found little of that sort of thing in such prospect holes as Parry's.

Mike lined up various lengths of drill steel near the face; then he came out of the drift and carried water up from the spring for a bath. While he washed he had water getting hot on the stove, and when he had finished he made coffee and a sandwich. He would have a good meal in town, but he knew from long experience that a man was foolish to start out for anywhere without eating something . . . too many things could happen.

And when he got to town he was going to see Wilson Hoyt first thing.

FIVE

Wilson Hoyt sat behind his battered roll-top desk, his feet propped up, reading a newspaper. He looked up as Mike Shevlin walked in, and acknowledged his presence with a brief nod and no show of pleasure.

"You've got something on your mind," he said bluntly. "What is it?"

"I'm going to blow the lid off, and I want you on my side."

Hoyt picked up the stub of his cigar and carefully ground it out before throwing it into the cuspidor. He should have known this job was too good to last.

Slowly and in detail, Mike Shevlin laid out the situation as he saw it. Ray Hollister was in that part of the country, and he had the cattlemen solidly behind him. The water of the creeks was being polluted, and the cattle needed that water. They would attack, the cattlemen would, and that meant killing and burning.

Ben Stowe would fight back, but regardless of who won, the town would lose. And, he added, Ben Stowe was robbing the mine owners.

"They don't live in Rafter," Hoyt said cynically, "so it doesn't matter." He bit the end from a fresh cigar. "How do you think it can be stopped?"

"Arrest Stowe. Arrest Mason and Gentry. Slap every man of them in jail, then go into the mines and get enough high-grade for evidence."

"What about Hollister?"

"Forget him. Bring in the five top ranchers and put them under bond to keep the peace. Then let Hollister stew in his own juice."

"They're outside my jurisdiction."

"Not if you want to act. Nobody really wants this trouble but Hollister. He's a sorehead."

Hoyt chewed the cigar thoughtfully, then took his feet down from the desk. "Now you listen to me. Nobody asked me to stop high-grading. I was brought in to keep the peace, and I've kept it. Now you come in here and try to tell me my business.

"If Ray Hollister starts anything, I'll kill him, and that goes for you as well. Ben Stowe won't start anything, because he needs peace and quiet. If you try to blow the lid off this town you're likely to get killed. And even if you started something, you couldn't prove a thing.

"Let me tell you something," Hoyt went on. "All the high-grade ore comes out of one area between the two mines. At the first sign of trouble, the drifts leading to the stopes where that high-grade ore has been found will be blown up and sealed off. You couldn't prove a thing, and you'd just make a fool of yourself."

Wilson Hoyt stood up. "Now you quit that two-bit job and get out of town. If you're still in town forty-eight hours from now, or if you so much as raise your voice, I'll come for you."

Shevlin felt angry with frustration and helplessness. This was the one man he needed, but if Hoyt persisted in his stand nothing could prevent killing. How could he reach him?

"You've heard my ultimatium," Hoyt said. "Get up in the saddle and start looking for distance."

"If you remembered me, Hoyt, you wouldn't be talking that way."

Hoyt brushed the remark off with a gesture. "Oh, I know all about you! You fought in the Nueces cattle war, you were a Texas Ranger for two years and made quite a name for yourself. You had a name around Cimarron and Durango. I know all that, and I'm not impressed."

Mike Shevlin tucked his thumbs behind his belt and said quietly, "I was remembering one night in Tascosa."

Wilson Hoyt's hands became very still. The leonine head was bowed slightly, the muscles in the powerful neck were rigid.

"It was bright moonlight," Mike said, "and you were under the cottonwoods waiting for a man, so when a rider came in from the Canadian River bottoms you were sure it was your man."

Hoyt's face was bleak.

"You stepped into the open, called out a name, and reached for your gun. Do you remember that?"

"I remember it."

"You were slow, Wilson. We'll say it was an off night. Anyway, this rider had the drop before your gun cleared leather, and when he spoke you knew you had braced the wrong man. Right so far?"

"Yes."

"There you stood looking into the muzzle of a gun in the hands of an unknown man, a man with every chance and every right to shoot you where you stood. Then the man walked his horse away and left you standing there, and you never knew who it was who beat you to the draw."

"You could have heard the story."

"I never told it."

"Well, you beat me once. That doesn't say you can do it again."

For years that faceless man had haunted Wilson Hoyt—that man whose features had been hidden by the shadows of his hat as well as by the trees. Now he knew.

"What's your stake in this? I'll not deny I owe you something. You could have shot me, yet you held your fire."

"Eli Patterson was my friend . . . that started it. Since then, something else has happened. I've been hired to stop the high-grading and recover the gold."

Hoyt swore. "Hired? Why'd they pick an outside man?"

Shevlin smiled. "You were keeping the peace, remember? You were letting things be, as long as everything was quiet."

Hoyt thrust the cigar back between his teeth. "I don't know about this. I got to think about it. You keep your shirt on, d'you hear?"

"Think fast then," Shevlin said. "I'm not smart, Hoyt. I only know one way—I walk right in swinging. By noon tomorrow I'm cutting my wolf loose, and if you're not with me you'd better hunt a hole."

In the neat red brick house with the white shutters that was the home of Dr. Rupert Clagg, late of Boston, they were having supper. The house itself, the neat green lawn, and the white picket fence were all indications of Dr. Clagg's quality of mind. He was himself neat, orderly, efficient.

Graduating at the top of his class from medical school, he could have stepped into a fine practice in any city in the East, but the War Between the States changed all that. After only a year in practice in Philadelphia, in the office of the city's most reputable physician, he had gone into the Army. The rough and ready life, the men he met, conspired to remove any latent desire to return to Philadelphia. Instead, he elected to go west.

Dottie Clagg was one of three daughters in one of Philadelphia's oldest and wealthiest families, but she possessed an adventurous spirit, and despite all the protests their two families could offer, they went west.

For a while Dr. Clagg had remained an Army surgeon, attached to various posts in New Mexico and Arizona. When he left the service a distant cousin, Clagg Merriam, who was in business in Rafter, suggested that they come there, and almost two years ago they had done so, prepared to settle down.

At thirty-four Dr. Rupert Clagg was erect, tall, and handsome, bronzed as any cowhand, and bearing an arrow scar on his cheekbone. His office was filled with frontier atmosphere, but his home remained a corner of the New England where he had been born.

He liked having people around, and had been pleased when Laine Tennison arrived to be their house guest. Laine and Dottie had attended school together in Philadelphia, and Dottie had been thrilled when Laine had written, mentioning coming west for her health.

"Although I don't know why," Dottie had confided to her husband. "She was always the picture of health."

"Maybe she just wants to get away."

"A love affair!" Dottie was at once delighted and positive. "She's had an unhappy love affair!"

"Laine?" Clagg was skeptical.

"Even a girl as beautiful as she is can be disappointed," Dottie protested.

Recognizing the fact that his wife could be as excited over an unhappy love affair as a happy one, he did not argue the point.

"I'm going to invite her for a visit," Dottie had said. "You don't mind, do you?"

"Mind? Laine? By all means invite her."

She had arrived a few weeks later and had proved an attentive listener to Dottie's endless chatter about people and happenings around Rafter. Laine, it seemed, was interested in all the trivia of life in a western mining town, and not the least bit bored.

Dr. Clagg offered few comments until Laine suggested that riding in the open air might be good for her health. Then he said, "By all means," and added, a shade wryly, "Just don't overdo it."

On this evening, when Clagg Merriam was also there for

supper, Dr. Rupert glanced at Laine across the table. "Your color is better," he said. "You were riding today?"

"Driving. I rented a buckboard from that nice old man at the livery stable and drove out past the Glory Hole."

"That nice old man," the doctor said ironically, "is a disreputable old outlaw."

"Really? He seems so sweet."

"I saw a new man in town today," Dottie said, "and a handsome devil, too. One of the big, rugged outdoor types. He was coming from the sheriff's office."

"Speaking of men," Dr. Clagg commented casually, "Ben Stowe was asking about you. He noticed you driving around alone and wondered who you were. He was most interested."

"You can't blame Ben," Clagg Merriam said. "After all, Miss Tennison is a very beautiful girl."

"Why, thank you, Mr. Merriam." Laine flashed him a quick smile. "But I am sure that wasn't the reason."

"He asked if you were from San Francisco," Dr. Rupert said, "but when I told him you were from Philadelphia he lost interest."

"Oh? So he doesn't like Philadelphia girls!" Dottie exclaimed. "You should have told him that Laine has an uncle in San Francisco . . . and a rich uncle, at that!"

Clagg Merriam glanced thoughtfully at Laine, but made no comment. Dr. Rupert, always an observant man, caught the expression on Laine's face. It had stiffened at Dottie's comment, and in the instant that Merriam looked at her, Laine shot Dottie a quick, protesting look.

Later, when the two men sat alone over brandy and cigars, Merriam commented, "Miss Tennison seems the picture of health. I think," he added judiciously, "that they caught hers in time."

"I wouldn't think it too safe for a girl to go riding around alone in a place like this. After all, the mines brought in all sorts of riffraff."

"She can look after herself, Clagg. And I believe the people here are quite stable. Remarkably stable, in fact. I also think most of them know she is my guest."

Walking away from the house an hour or so later, Clagg Merriam wondered whether Dr. Rupert's last comment had been a warning of some kind.

After he had left, Dr. Rupert sat in his big chair and lighted his pipe. Laine had asked for no medical advice, but he was as sure as one could be without a physical examination that there was nothing in the world wrong with Laine Tennison.

Which left the question: What was she doing in Rafter, of all places? A broken heart? Absurd. Laine was often thoughtful, but she never moped.

Ben Stowe had been curious, even prying. And Dottie's remark about an uncle in San Francisco had stirred immediate interest in Merriam. Only a fool would need to ask why. Rafter was motivated by only one idea, the gold from the mines. And who owned the mines? Some interests in San Francisco.

Every day Laine rode out, or drove, and as often as not she traveled the back trails. Was it just out of curiosity, or for some other, more definite reason?

Ben Stowe seemed suspicious, and if, as Dr. Rupert thought, she was connected with the ownership of the mines, then she could be in real trouble.

Old Brazos at the livery stable was known to Dr. Rupert. It was the doctor who had treated a badly infected leg wound when the old outlaw first rode into Rafter, and he had mentioned it to no one. He liked the hard-bitten old man, and was liked in return.

Now, as he packed tobacco into his pipe, he thought that he must have a talk with Brazos, for little went on around town that the old hostler did not know. And Laine Tennison was his guest, and must be protected.

The doctor had never accepted more than a fair price for his medical attentions, and he had always refused to be paid in gold. His attitude in this was known, and he had never been bothered. Was that because he was respected? Because they needed a good doctor in town? Or because he was Clagg Merriam's cousin? For Clagg Merriam was a man of some authority in Rafter.

Of course, there was a simpler reason. Dr. Rupert was notoriously close-mouthed—everybody in town knew it. But how much would that help if it was discovered that Laine Tennison had some connection with the Sun Strike?

He considered that while he smoked his pipe out, carefully examining all aspects of the problem. At the end of the evening one thing was clear: From now on, Laine Tennison was in danger.

How many of the corrupted citizens of Rafter had been corrupted enough to stand by if it came to doing harm to a young girl? If it came to murder, even? Would they look the other way? How many would actually condone murder to protect what they had?

He knocked out his pipe and walked across the room to the

rifle rack. Carefully, he checked every weapon. And then he took his Army Colt, checked the loads, and tucked it behind his waistband.

From this moment, Dr. Rupert Clagg would go armed.

SIX

When Mike Shevlin had walked out of Wilson Hoyt's office several hours earlier, he was jumpy as a cat that smells snake.

His every instinct warned him that time was running out both for himself and for Laine Tennison. The fact that she was Eli Patterson's niece had bought his loyalty as no offer of a share in the gold could have done; although, being a practical man, he was not unaware of what ten per cent of perhaps half a million dollars could mean in cattle.

He paused on a corner of the street, staring about like a bull entering a bullring, searching for something at which to charge.

He needed to find the gold cache, and to be able to prevent them removing it when panic set in. His instinct told him the proper thing was to bust right into the middle of things and start things happening. It was a good way to get hurt, but from experience he knew that when a nest of crooks is disturbed they are apt to move without planning, and so make mistakes they might not otherwise make.

It was for this reason that he had deliberately prodded Wilson Hoyt. Any move the marshal might make at this time would help. Even if he only started asking questions it might be enough.

While Shevlin stood there, Ben Stowe suddenly appeared in the door of the Nevada House, and Mike Shevlin started toward him, walking swiftly. Stowe turned at the sound of his heels, and Shevlin caught the hard, measuring look. And suddenly Mike felt like old times. He knew that now the waiting was over and he was going into battle. He felt a wild surge of eagerness within him that he had to fight down.

Stowe was poised and ready for him. Mike saw it even as

Stowe spoke. "Hello, Mike. How about a drink for old times' sake?"

"No time for drinking, Ben." Mike grinned at him, daringly, challengingly. "I'm going to tear down your playhouse, Ben."

Ben Stowe's expression did not change; he simply said, "Mike, everybody would be happier if you'd just ride on out of here." Ben reached in his pocket and took out a fat roll of bills. "Now, if you're short of cash—?"

"Remember me? There were always a lot of things more important than money."

"Eli Patterson is dead, Mike. If you start opening that up, a lot of people will get hurt."

"That's what I had in mind."

"You won't leave?"

Ben Stowe was thinking about his plans for Shevlin. The trouble was, they might not work fast enough, so he'd have to make other, faster plans.

"Ben?" Mike spoke quietly, almost gently, so that suddenly every sense in Stowe's body was alert. "Ben, why don't *you* leave?"

Stowe was startled at the words. He stared sharply, unbelievingly at Shevlin. "*Me?* Why should I leave?"

"Think about it, Ben. You and me, we're not exactly tenderfeet. We've both been through the mill. I say, grab it and run. You've had everything your way, and you've got a lot stashed away, so why not take it and get out? Believe me, Ben, it's all over."

Ben Stowe started to make an angry reply, then hesitated. Shevlin was keyed up, he could see that, and the last thing Stowe wanted was a gun battle. And then he had a shocking sense that Shevlin was right.

He struck a match and took his time lighting his cigar. He was shocked at the sudden wave of panic that had swept through him.

Ben Stowe was realist enough to know that the doubt had been lingering there all the time, and Shevlin's words had just exploded his feeling into desperation. In any such deal as this there was always that feeling that it was too good to last; and that feeling had been building larger and larger in all of them. Only a damned fool could fail to be apprehensive. But Ben Stowe was a hard man; he fought down his panic.

"You seem to be riding a rough saddle, Mike. What's your stake in all this?"

"Give me the man who killed Eli."

Stowe shot him a swift glance. "Eli? Mike, men have died

before, and others have yet to die, so why get worked up over him?"

He made one last attempt, not to buy Shevlin, but to stall him. "Why not come into the party, Mike? This cake is big enough for all of us."

"Give me the man who killed Eli."

Stowe drew on his cigar. "Now, I might just do that, Mike," he said, knowing he could do nothing of the kind. "Give me a couple of days."

"Make it twenty-four hours." Shevlin moved to be off. "But take it from me, Ben, you'd better take what you've got and run. Your game's played out."

Abruptly, he walked away. Ben Stowe would be no bargain in a fight. He had always been tough, but he was tougher, colder, and smarter now.

Somehow he must crack the tight ring that Stowe had built around the enterprise. Once that ring was cracked, once somebody was hit with panic, then the whole thing would fall apart as everybody scrambled for safety with everything they could lay their hands on.

Mason . . . Mason had to be the weak link. Not Gib Gentry, for Gib would dig in his heels and make a fight of it. Nor did Mike wish to tangle with Gib—they had eaten too much dust and alkali together. Crack Mason, and Gentry would get out fast; and after Mason, Stowe would have to make his fight.

Mike Shevlin was no fool. Pausing briefly on the corner, he knew he was looking at an uncertain future. He was forcing things into the open now, but it was the only way he knew how to act. Let the others play it cosy; he had neither the time nor the patience.

First, he had to get Laine Tennison out of town before the roof fell in. Even without that, he would have enough trouble taking care of himself.

Bleakly, he thought of tomorrow, and knew that tomorrow's sun might not shine upon his face. For he was walking into more trouble than he had ever tackled in his life, and he had no friends. He was alone, as he had always been alone. And he would die alone, die somewhere up a canyon when his shells ran out, or his canteen was empty and his horse dead.

He had always known that was the way it would be. It was hell, when a man came to think of it. He'd never felt sorry for himself, but right now there wasn't a soul anywhere in the world who would think of it twice if he was killed. There was nobody who cared; and the odd part of it was, there never had been, as long as he could recall.

He had brushed aside such thoughts before; what was bringing them to mind now? Was there deep within him a realization of death? Was he really going to pay it out now?

He had never been in love, and so far as he knew he had never been loved by a woman. Here and there he had known women, some of them with affection, but it had gone no deeper than that. He knew he was a one-woman man, and had always known it; and he shied away now from the face that appeared sharply before his eyes. Not for him. Not for such as he, was a girl like Laine Tennison.

In the back of his mind there had always been the vague idea that someday he would find the girl he was looking for. He would buy himself a nice little spread, fix it up shipshape and cosy, and maybe they'd have a couple of youngsters. . . . He was a hell of a person to have such ideas.

Mike Shevlin considered the present situation with care. He had really kicked over the applecart, and no mistake. Wilson Hoyt would not sit still. He would at least make inquiries, try to take some steps to avoid trouble. That Ben Stowe would also take steps would be quite in keeping with the man as he remembered him.

At the livery stable Shevlin got his horse and rode out of town, then circled around and came up behind Dr. Rupert Clagg's place. There were tall cottonwoods behind the house, rustling their leaves in the faint stir of air.

Swinging down, he tied his horse well into the deepest shadow of the trees. He must see Laine. He must warn her, and he must get her out of town if possible.

He moved toward the house and paused by a thick old tree, listening into the night. From the kitchen came the faint clatter of dishes and the momentary sound of a girl's voice lifted in talk.

Something stirred in the grass near him, and a moment later a voice spoke. "All right, what do you want?"

"I want to see Laine Tennison."

"Rather late for that, isn't it? If she knows you and wishes to see you, come around tomorrow."

Laine's voice interrupted. "It is all right, Rupert. I want to see him."

Mike Shevlin lifted the latch of the gate and came into the back yard. The light in the kitchen had been blown out, and the rear of the house was dark. He stood uncertainly inside the gate. "All right," the man's voice said, "if Miss Tennison wishes to see you." There was a pause. "I am Dr. Clagg."

Shevlin turned his head, listening for any sound of a possible ambush. "Related to Clagg Merriam?" he asked.

"A distant cousin."

"Ah?"

"Will you come into the house?"

Mike hesitated, then followed them into the house. They went through the dark kitchen and along a lighted hall into a comfortable living room.

"Drink?"

"No, thanks."

Dr. Rupert and Mike Shevlin measured each other. "Coffee?" the doctor suggested. "We're tea drinkers ourselves, but we always have coffee."

"I'll have tea," Mike said. "I spent a winter one time in a horse camp with an Englishman. I got to like it."

Laine had come into the room and Clagg turned to go. "I'll let you talk," he said. "I must tell Dottie what's going on."

"You stay." Shevlin did not mean to speak so abruptly, but he suddenly realized that Clagg was a solid citizen, and a fighting man. "You'd better hear this. You'll know it all in a day or so, anyway."

Dottie came down the stairs and into the room. "Ma'am," Shevlin said, "I'm Mike Shevlin, and all hell's about to break loose."

SEVEN

Ben Stowe chewed angrily on his cigar. That damned, gun-handy saddle tramp, drifting in here to ruin everything! Why couldn't he have stayed in Texas, or wherever he had come from?

The years bring about many changes in the characters of men. Gib Gentry had always been a careless, rough-and-ready cowhand, never too honest in any dealings, yet a man who was, generally speaking, without malice. He had never stolen anything but cattle, and the West looked with tolerance upon branding loose stock. If a man happened to be so unlucky as to be caught in the act, he would probably be hung or shot, but it was generally understood that any maverick was taking its own chances as long as there was a running iron, a cinch ring, or a twist of barbed wire lying about handy.

Gib Gentry, who appreciated a good joke, had once made the rounds of a roundup camp and surreptitiously checked all the saddles. Of the forty men present—ranchers, cowhands, and stock inspectors—thirty-one of them had cinch rings on their saddles that showed signs of fire. At the time it caused considerable embarrassment, followed by a run on the nearest harness shops for extra cinch rings, but afterward it became a standing joke on the range.

In Gentry's book, high-grading gold was not too far afield from cattle rustling. The gold was in the earth, the fact of discovery was an accident; why shouldn't he profit as well as the next man? Neither kind of theft disturbed whatever moral code Gib possessed . . . either kind was taken for granted, and nothing more thought of it.

But the murder of Jack Moorman was something else, and Gib had never really gotten over that. No ghosts haunted him

54

in the night, and he carried no aura of guilt, visible to himself or others. He simply drank a little more, ate a little more, softened up physically a little faster, and avoided the subject even in his own mind. Whenever the memory of old Jack's brutal killing came to him he quickly averted his thoughts and tried to think of something else. As there was a very busty young Irish waitress down at the restaurant called The Sump, he found this a relatively easy thing to do.

Ben Stowe was another kind of man entirely. He, too, was without malice in whatever he had done. He would have laughed at the idea that society owed him a living, or owed him anything. Gentry was reckless, immature, and took what he wanted; Stowe was cold, calculating, intelligent, and thought the law was for damned fools.

As Gentry had deteriorated, Stowe had grown in evil. As he was cold, so he had become colder; as he was a thinking man, he had become an executive in crime, which he conducted as any business operation should be conducted. He was utterly ruthless.

He would never murder a man just for the sake of killing. He would never indulge in rape or in casual theft. He would have fallen into few of the categories that fit criminal types. He was simply a totally selfish man with a complete disregard for the rights of others to either life or property, if in some way these rights interfered with his own plans.

Once his mind was made up, he wasted no time. And his mind was made up now about Mike Shevlin.

He had planned that Shevlin should die, but he had planned to arrange it to happen in such a way as no blame could attach itself to the town or to anybody in it. There were ways to do such things, and he had used them before. Now there was no time for that.

Turning on his heel, he walked back to the Nevada House and into the saloon. Red was there, as Stowe had known he would be. Red was never far from people, for he was too much involved in a romance with the sound of his own voice.

Stowe caught his eyes, and Red came over. Stowe bought drinks for both of them.

"There's a man out at Boulder Spring," he said. "You ride out there. Say nothing of this to anybody . . . not to anybody at all. You just ride out there and tell him to scratch the first name."

When Red was gone, Ben Stowe took his bottle and walked to a corner table. Now he must think. Every move must be planned.

The ledgers in his office told him just what each mine was taking out, and each was permitted to show a small profit occasionally. There was another book he kept hidden that told of each deposit of gold in the cache.

Now, like it or not, they were going to have to ship some of the gold to an eastern market. Stowe had made plans for this over a year ago. Gentry would handle the shipment, and it would arrive at the eastern market as though shipped from another mine than this.

Money was necessary to continue the operation of the plan, and they must have sufficient capital to make a payment on the purchase price of the mine if a deal could be arrived at. It was unfortunate that Mike Shevlin had appeared at this time with his talk of blowing the lid off, but he would be out of the picture within a matter of hours.

Stowe sat quietly, smoking his cigar and thinking, considering every aspect of the loading of the gold, the route the shipment must take, and its protection en route, without it seeming to be protected.

The next few days would settle the affair. The shipment, if the timing was to be right, must leave within the next forty-eight hours.

Only yesterday he had given that list to the man at Boulder Spring, a list of five men to be shot on order, and they were five men carefully selected. He considered that again, wondering if there were others, but he could think of none. All but one of those whose names were on that list would have been shocked to realize that such a thing could be; and not one, Stowe told himself, would suspect it of him. Of them all, Mike Shevlin might guess his own name was there, but none of the others could imagine themselves on such a list.

Gib Gentry was finishing his third drink at the bar of the Blue Horn Saloon when Red pushed through the doors and came up to the bar beside him.

Gib had been staring at his image in the mirror without pleasure. All the fun had gone out of things lately, and he might as well face up to the fact that he was no longer a youngster.

He was nearing forty . . . oh, there were a couple of years to go, but a man had to face the fact that he was closing in on it. He owned a stage line with two vehicles and a steady business, and a freight line operating sixteen big wagons, with barns and corrals at each end. He was making money.

Ben Stowe was his silent partner, but he took no pleasure in that. More and more he had realized in these past few days that after ten years of association with Ben he did not like him, and did not really know him. But to pull out and leave all he owned, and start over at his age—well, that made no sense, either.

Like many another man in his position, he allowed himself to remain tied to a situation that worried him, and only because of the little property it represented. He brooded while he sat there drinking, and he had just refilled his glass when Red entered the door.

Irritated, for he wished to be alone, Gentry said, "You'd better watch your step. You took in too much territory the other day."

The taunt had a bite, but Red chuckled, though without humor. "Maybe, but he won't be pullin' that on me again . . . not him."

"He could murder you in any kind of a fight. I know him."

Resentment fought with caution, and resentment won for the moment. "He ain't goin' to bother me, nor anybody else for that matter. Not any more, he ain't. He's had it."

Gentry's glass described a slow circle on the bar. Through his brain, dulled by whiskey, the idea filtered slowly. He started to ask a question, then restrained himself. If he questioned Red, the miner would simply clam up and he would get nothing from him, nothing at all. Yet he had a feeling Red wanted to talk—he wanted to brag about how much he knew.

"Don't you go counting on that. Shevlin will be around for a good long spell."

Red had some remnants of caution, but he did want to talk and he knew that no one was closer to Ben Stowe than Gentry; so it certainly could do no harm to tell him.

He downed his drink. "Not after I come back from Boulder Spring, he won't be. Not for long. He'll have a day, maybe two or three."

Red was guessing, but he had a feeling he wasn't missing the mark very far. He had seen Shevlin exchange some angry words with Stowe, and after that had come the message. And he knew that Shevlin was causing trouble . . . by now everyone in town knew that.

Suddenly another thought came to Red. Stowe had said, "Scratch the first name."

The *first* name? That implied there was a list, it implied there were more names. If Shevlin's was the first name on the list, whose were the other names?

"That Ben," Red confided, "he's a cagey one. Always knows what he's about."

Gentry was silent, thinking of Red's information. So the word was out—Shevlin was to be killed.

Anger filled him. Ben was a damned fool. Djdn't he know a man like Mike Shevlin would take a lot of killing?

There were some who might low-rate Mike Shevlin, but Gentry was not one of them. He had always known there was a tiger in Shevlin, and he had seen it loosed a time or two. And this Shevlin who had come back to Rafter was a far cry from the tough but unseasoned boy who had left.

Red was a stupid man, and a talkative, boastful man. As he finished his second drink he realized that he held an enormous piece of information, and it was too much for him. Deep within. him he understood that he should repeat nothing of what he knew—but wasn't Gentry one of the outfit?

"Gib," he said, leaning closer, "you don't figure me for knowing anything, but I bet I know something you don't. Ben has him a little list, a death list. And Shevlin is number one on that list."

Red put down his glass, waiting for some kind of reply, but Gentry waited, seeming to ignore him.

"You'll see, when Shevlin turns up missing."

Red walked outside, the batwing doors swinging behind him. Within a few minutes he would be on his way, and he would have forgotten his loose-tongued talk. But Gentry would not forget it, for Gentry knew who was at Boulder Spring.

He had stumbled on the knowledge by accident, and had kept it to himself. He had used his head in not mentioning it to Stowe, but now he realized that he was starting a bit late to use his head.

He was, he reflected bitterly, just beginning to grow up, and he was coming to realize that he had spent most of his life being something of a damned fool. When the country was overrun with cattle, many of doubtful ownership, it had been fun to brand a few head, drive them to some out-of-the-way market, and then spend the money on a big wing-ding—riding horses into saloons and shooting out a few street lamps or windows had been part of the fun. And when the high-grading started it had seemed no different from the rustling.

Befuddled with drink as he was, his mind began to gnaw slowly at the problem, puzzling over it in a way he never would have done if cold sober. Red had said that Shevlin was first on that list, but who else was listed?

Ray Hollister?

He sorted around in his mind for other names. Shevlin and

Hollister, both logical enough. But a *list* implied more than two. Who, then, were the others?

Gentry himself was to come in for a large share of that high-graded gold when it was finally disposed of . . . but suppose, just suppose, that his name was also on that list?

He tossed off the rest of his drink and turned from the bar. His shoulder collided with the doorjamb as he went out, lurching across the walk to the edge, where he stared up the darkening street.

That man out at Boulder Spring was Lon Court. Gentry, who fancied himself good with a gun, was simply a hell-for-leather, draw-and-blast-'em type of fighter. Lon Court was a killer for pay. He was a meat-hunter, a man who worked with a long-range rifle and careful planning, who killed the way some men branded stock or stacked wheat. He was cold, deadly, and efficient.

Standing alone on the empty street, Gentry suddenly knew he was no longer in a quandry. For the first time, his life held definite purpose.

In that stark moment on the street his mind cleared. When most men had gone to their suppers he stood there alone, and was aware of his aloneness; and he realized that in all his careless, heedless young manhood the closest thing to a friend he had ever had was Mike Shevlin.

The rest of the old crowd were gone. They had drifted away, become family men, or had been killed at work or died at the end of a rope or by the gun. He and Shevlin were the only ones left.

There was Ben Stowe, of course, but where the others had been wild and reckless, Ben had always been cold and ruthless, working for every last buck, and the hell with anybody who got in the way.

Of just one thing Gentry was sure now. Mike Shevlin was too good a man to be shot from ambush by a man like Lon Court. He strode down the street to the livery stable and claimed his horse.

"You seen Shevlin?" he asked Brazos. His speech was thick, but to himself his purpose was clear. "I got to see him. Right away."

Brazos threw him a sharp glance. Gentry was drunk, yes, but he wasn't fighting drunk. What showed in his eyes was anxiety, not animosity.

"He headed out toward Parry's claim," Brazos said. "Over in the box canyon."

Gentry stepped into the saddle and rode into the night.

Drunk or sober, he had always been able to ride anything he could get astride of. Now the night air began to clear his whiskey-fogged mind. One thing stood out; Lon Court had a little list.

Shevlin, Hollister, Babcock . . . who else? Why, you damned fool, he told himself, your name will be on that list!

After all, what was he to Stowe? There had never been any sentiment in Stowe, but always plenty of greed; and now when Gentry's mind was capable of thinking, and he remembered that his own share of that gold would come to more than a hundred thousand dollars, he had the answer. Ben Stowe wouldn't share that kind of money with anybody.

Somebody, Gentry had never known who, must have mort-gaged everything he owned to put up the cash to buy the gold from the stores, an operation handled by Stowe himself. Only Stowe, his unknown backer, Ray Hollister, and Gentry himself knew the setup.

Ben Stowe had been hot to have Hollister hunted down and killed; then it would surely be Gentry's turn. After that, who would be the next target in the shooting gallery?

EIGHT

The soft desert night, dark beneath the stars, seemed still, yet it was a night of restlessness, a night of movement.

Ben Stowe had returned to his desk, irritable at the necessity for rearranging plans because of Mike Shevlin, but not actually worried by it. Within an hour Lon Court would have his message, and the message called for immediate action.

In his room in the jail building, Wilson Hoyt lay awake. He had made his final rounds, and all had been in order, yet his instinct warned him that behind the soft darkness and the quiet, trouble stirred.

Throughout his life he had ridden on the side of the law. Of course, in every community where he had held office there were certain things he was expected to overlook, because the town gave its tacit consent to them. There had been towns where men carried guns because it was the thing to do; there were other towns, in more thickly settled communities, where guns were not allowed to be carried, and in those towns he had forbidden strangers to carry them within the city limits.

His role, as he saw it, was not to take care of morals but to keep the peace. In a life on the frontier he had come to accept rough living by rough men, and he interfered only when such a way of living threatened the peace of the town and its citizens. He was here to prevent disorderly conduct, within reason, to prevent theft or murder, and to punish the offenders if such things were attempted or carried out. Here, the town had accepted high-grading as a fact of its community life, so he had done the same.

He had been warned that a man named Ray Hollister would come to town one day and try to cause trouble, and he had been told that Hollister was a dangerous man. Wilson Hoyt had checked the records and the memories of Hollister and had found this to be true. The man was undoubtedly a troublemaker.

But now this man Shevlin had appeared in town and had laid it on the line for him. Wilson Hoyt knew that the time had come when he must take a stand.

Trouble was surely here. It was being brought about by high-grading, and the peace of his town, quiet until now, was to be ripped apart. Shevlin had given him a choice, and Wilson Hoyt lay awake this night, trying to make up his mind what to do—and how to do it.

His instinct, and his better judgment too, told him that the thing to do was to end the high-grading and deliver the gold to its owners. He would, of course, promptly be fired, but that did not especially disturb him. He had been hunting a job when he had found this one. He could look for one again.

As Hoyt lay on his cot trying to make up his mind, Ben Stowe chewed on a dead cigar; and at Dr. Rupert Clagg's, Mike Shevlin was sitting down at a table with the doctor, his wife and daughter, and Laine Tennison.

Not many miles away, Red was arriving at Boulder Spring with a message for Lon Court; and Gib Gentry, wishing to warn his friend, was taking the trail to Burt Parry's claim.

Ben Stowe foresaw no interruption in his plans that could last more than a few days. Shevlin was a dangerous obstacle, but Lon Court would remove that obstacle smoothly and efficiently. Ray Hollister was somewhere around, but the ranches of his friends were watched day and night, and when he was located he would be picked up.

But even as he sat alone in his office, Ben Stowe had no way of knowing that there was a meeting at the Three Sevens.

The ranch house was ablaze with lights, and Hollister was there, seated at the head of the table. Eve Bancroft was watching him with admiring eyes; Babcock loitered at the back of the room. The others at the table were ranchers or their foremen, and they were listening to Hollister.

On the rugged slope of the mountain, half a mile or more away, Ben Stowe's watcher lay sprawled on his back staring at the stars with wide-open, unblinking eyes. There was little about him that resembled anything human, for he had been roped and dragged for two miles along the rough mountain through broken lava and cactus, bunch grass and cat-claw. Ray Hollister had done the dragging, then had shaken loose his loop and ridden away. Babcock, more merciful, had paused by the man who looked up at him, ruined beyond recovery, but still conscious. "That draggin' wasn't my idea," Babcock said, and fired the bullet that put the dying man beyond misery.

The riders at the Three Sevens all wore guns. On their horses there were Winchesters. They had come prepared to attack the monster that was destroying their cattle business. They would blow up the mine and drive out Ben Stowe and his crew; then the ranchers' water would be pure again, their business would once more be the focal occupation of the Rafter country.

They were, on the whole, honest, forthright men, protecting their livelihood by the only means they knew, protecting, as they believed, their range land from destruction. They were men born to a life of violence, men who did not approve of violence but who had been led to its use by a fanatic, a fanatic who was also an envious, embittered man, fighting tooth and nail for a position in the world that nothing fitted him to hold.

Dr. Rupert Clagg faced Mike Shevlin across the table, over their teacups. Dottie and Laine sat with them.

Dr. Clagg, who had seen others like Mike Shevlin in many places in the West, knew what a force such a man could be. On his occasional journeys back to the East, he had become impatient with those who spoke with tolerant smiles of the West, or of what they referred to as "the western myth." Back of every myth there is a stern, harsh reality shaped by men and women of truly heroic mold. Those soft-bellied ones who come later find it easy to refer to things beyond their own grasp as myth; but the men Dr. Clagg had known were men who created myth every day of their lives, usually without any consciousness of doing so, but quite often with awareness that they were experiencing a life that was extraordinary.

Dr. Clagg had been in Dodge when the twenty-eight buffalo hunters, who made the fight at Adobe Walls against more than a thousand Indians, returned from their fight. He was familiar, as were all western men, with the escape of John Coulter from the Blackfoot Indians, a run compared to which the run from the battlefield of Marathon pales to insignificance. He knew the story of Hugh Glass and the grizzly; the story of the ride of Portugee Phillips through a raging blizzard and thousands of Indians to bring help to Fort Phil Kearny; and he knew well the story of the Alamo.

The stuff of which such myths are made was born every day

in the West, but at the moment of birth they were not myth; they were hard reality, the very stuff of life itself.

Dr. Rupert Clagg, who was more of such a man as these than he himself realized, recognized another in Mike Shevlin.

"I'm sorry to be so blunt," Shevlin said, "but there's no other way of putting it. Ma'am,"—he turned to Laine—"I want you to leave town. I want you out of here on the first stage in the morning, at the latest, but I'd prefer that you'd let me drive you out in a buckboard before daybreak."

"It's as serious as that?" Clagg asked.

Mike Shevlin outlined the situation as he saw it. He told them what he had done about both Ben Stowe and Wilson Hoyt.

"And the gold?" asked the doctor. "You still don't know where it is?"

"No. I've got a hunch, but it doesn't shape up to much. Only I think they'll make a break to get it out of here. I think they will figure it had better go now, for they may not get another chance any time soon. And they won't."

"I will not go." Laine Tennison spoke firmly. "I have business here, and I refuse to be run out of town. I shall stay right here and see it through."

"Now listen—" Mike began.

"I'm sorry, Mr. Shevlin." She smiled suddenly. "I think you knew all the time that I wouldn't go, although I know you had to try. . . . No, I shall stay."

She glanced at his cup. "Mr. Shevlin, you aren't drinking your tea."

He gulped it down, burning his mouth a little, and wanted to swear, but refrained.

"You do not know who is in this with Stowe?" Clagg asked.

"I have an idea."

"Clagg Merriam?"

Shevlin looked hard at Dr. Rupert. "That's who I had in mind."

"So had I," Clagg said, and added, "My remote cousin has always been well off. But I know he has been strapped for money for some time now, and he is not the man to mortgage anything unless the return promises to be more than adequate."

For a few minutes, nobody spoke. They sipped their tea in silence, and then Laine said, "Mr. Shevlin, I am afraid I am going to discharge you."

"Why?"

"You mustn't risk your life for me."

He grinned at her. "Ma'am, you've made a mistake. I am not

risking it for you, but for ten per cent of half a million dollars, and for Eli Patterson." His eyes twinkled. "Although I'd say if I was planning on risking my life for anybody, you'd be about the prettiest reason I could find."

Laine flushed, but she was not to be turned aside. "A foolish reason, Mr. Shevlin. A girl would want a live man, not a dead one."

"We have simple feelings out here, Miss Tennison," Shevlin said. "We're not a complicated folk. If a man wants to be bad or mean out here in the West, there's not much to stop him if he's big enough and tough enough to get away with it.

"On the other hand, if a man is honest it is because he wants to be. It isn't like back east, where there's the law and all. Out here there's mighty little gray, it is black or white, because there's no restraint, not even much in the way of public opinion—except as to cowardice or the value of a man's word.

"And when it comes to a fight, a man can't walk away from it if he's made it his fight. Not and continue to live in the West. You would want a live man, I'm sure, but you'd also want one who lived up to what he believed. Ma'am, I think this here is my fight now, just as much as it's yours, and I don't want a dime of your pay."

He got up and took up his hat. "I'm going out there now and build the biggest fire anybody ever built. I'm going to bust everything wide open and scatter the pieces so far Mr. Ben Stowe will never be able to put them together again.

"I'm not a smart man, Miss Tennison, so I'm going to charge in, head down and swinging: You just keep out of the way."

Brazos was dozing in his chair when Shevlin came up to the door of the stable. Startled, the old hostler stared up at him.

"You see Gib Gentry? He started out your way, a-huntin' you."

"I didn't go out there." Shevlin glanced up the dark street, then stepped into the stable, away from the light. He had left his horse a few yards up the street in the shadows.

"Brazos, where does Mason live?" he asked.

Brazos looked at him slowly, carefully, then indicated an alley across the street. "About a hundred yards back of that alley, in a long shack with three windows on this side. You can't miss it."

"Thanks," Shevlin stepped outside.

"He won't be alone," Brazos spoke after him. "Deek Taylor will be with him." Deek Taylor was a tough man, a very tough man.

Mike Shevlin mounted his horse and rode across the street

and up the alley. He stopped near the long cabin and got down. He went up to the door and tried it. It did not open, so he put a shoulder against it and smashed in.

"Who the hell is that?" Mason's voice said sleepily.

Shevlin stood to the right of the door, listening. He had heard a sharp cessation of breathing somewhere ahead of him. "Strike a light," he said. "I want to talk."

But at the same moment he struck a match himself, and saw a coal-oil lamp on the table before him. Lifting the still warm chimney, he touched the match to the wick. Mason had his head lifted and was blinking at him.

Shevlin looked toward the other occupied bunk. Deek Taylor, a lean, lantern-jawed man with hard eyes, was there and he was looking at Shevlin with no pleasure.

"I'm talking to *him*," Shevlin said, jerking a thumb at Mason. "Are you in this or out of it?"

"Well, now, that depends."

"Not a damn' bit, it doesn't. You speak up now. If you're in it, you can have a belly full. If you're out of it, you keep your trap shut and lie quiet and you won't get hurt."

"Hurt?" Taylor swung his legs to the floor. "Well, now—"

As his feet hit the floor, Mike Shevlin grabbed the front of his long-johns and jerked him up out of the bunk. As he jerked, he swung a rock-hard fist. Taylor tried to straighten up, he tried to turn, but the fist smashed him on the jaw, and again in the face, then jerked him back to meet the punches. A hard slug in the belly pushed him into a corner.

"If you're smart," Shevlin said, "you'll lie quiet and hope I forget about you."

He turned toward Mason. The gambler was staring, white-faced, and wide awake now. "Say, who the hell—?" And then Shevlin's face was in the light, and for the first time Mason saw who the visitor was.

"Mike! Mike Shevlin!"

"Sure." Mike dropped on the edge of Taylor's bunk, glancing once toward the man with the bloody face who lay sprawled in the corner. "You should have known I'd be back, Mase. Now you tell me: *Who killed Eli Patterson?*"

Mason had picked up the stub of a cigar and he tried to strike a match to it, but the match broke. He tried again, his hand shaking. Mason had never been a brave man.

"Now, Mike, you know I—"

"Mase," Shevlin said quietly, "you saw what just happened to Taylor. I'd have to work you over a damn' sight worse, and I haven't got time. Tell me who killed Eli, and then you can ride."

He struck a match and held it to Mason's cigar.

"Gentry," Mason began, "he—"

"Gentry took the blame, and he lied. Now you tell me who he lied for. You tell me, Mase, and you've got a running start." He gestured toward the street. "You got any idea what's going on out there tonight?" he went on. "Hollister's back. He's got the ranchers with him. They'll come in and they'll get hell shot out of them, but Stowe will get hurt, too. Then Hoyt and me, we'll pick up the pieces."

He wished it would be that easy. Ray Hollister's timing was always bad, and it would be this time too. And Hoyt might not make up his mind fast enough, which would leave somebody in the middle holding a handful of deuces.

And that somebody would be Mike Shevlin.

NINE

Mason hesitated, his lips trembling. He remembered Mike Shevlin, but this was a different man from the one he had known. This Mike Shevlin was bigger, stronger, tougher. He was a man of decision, and Mason had just had an object lesson in that. What Taylor might have done had he gotten into action was not the question, for he had been put out of action swiftly and efficiently. And Mason was no Deek Taylor.

He thought of his horse. It was close by, in the stable only a few yards back of the house. The pickings had been good, and he had been wise enough to keep his take cached near the town, for he had always known there would be a time for running, just as there always had been before this. And the time had come now. Only he had been a long time in Rafter, and he wanted to stay. They had protected him here because he had protected them.

"Mike," he protested, "you got to believe this. I don't know."

"Don't give me that."

"Honest to God, Mike! They needed a witness, and I was paid to swear that Gentry did it."

"Who paid you?"

"Mike, you aren't going to believe this, but it was Gib. It was Gentry himself."

Shevlin glanced over at Taylor. The man was moaning, and was clutching what was apparently a broken jaw. Mike's eyes returned to Mason.

"So?"

"That's all I know—I swear it, Mike! Gentry paid me."

"And you've no idea?"

Mason hesitated, and then he shrugged. "Mike, I swear that's all I know."

68

"Ben didn't do it?"

"No, not Ben. At least, I don't think it was Ben. Not that he'd hesitate. Gentry didn't do it either. Gentry was close to Ben, so there for a while I figured . . .

"But the last thing they wanted was any kind of an investigation. They wanted the whole thing cleared up, whitewashed and off the boards. Figure it for yourself, if somebody came in and started asking questions, somebody might slip up and the whole shooting match would go down the drain.

"That there Ben—I never knew he had it in him. He worked almighty fast, and you never saw things handled like that."

Mason's confidence was returning. "Mike, what's going to happen? You say Hollister's back and about to blow things up? Well, who takes over when the shooting's finished?"

He started to get up. "Mike, why not you and me? I know how these things work, and—"

Shevlin looked at him coldly. "How much do you know? You haven't told me anything yet." He paused. "Where's the gold?"

Mason glanced at him slyly. "Now, there's a good question. Where *is* the gold? There hasn't been an ounce leave this town, you can bank on that."

Mike Shevlin was listening beyond the house, his ears attuned to street movement. Was tonight the night?

"If you know anything, talk." Shevlin spoke shortly. He was wasting his time here. Hell might break loose at any moment.

"How about our deal?" Mason persisted. "How about—"

"No deal. You talk now, or by God, I'll—"

He grabbed Mason by the shirt front and jerked him to his feet. Then he shoved him against the wall near the door with force enough to shake the house. He started for him, and Mason threw up both hands.

"Don't hit me, for God's sake, Mike!"

"Then talk!"

"All I know is that part of it wasn't set up by Ben. It was set up by Evans."

"Evans?"

Shevlin was startled. Evans was the shyster lawyer with whom Ray Hollister had been a partner.

Evans?

He suddenly realized several things, all at once. But there was a question to be answered. "Where is Evans?" he asked. "What happened to him?"

Mason chuckled. "Now there *is* a question. What did happen to him? Seems that about the time they ran Ray out of town, Evans went too. Or so they say. Nobody saw him go, and Evans wasn't the type to run."

There was no use wasting any more time here. Mike Shevlin turned toward the door. "Mason, take my advice and get out of town. You're on short time here—you delay a little bit and you'll be caught right in the middle of it."

Shevlin went out and closed the door behind him.

The town was dark, and it was silent, but the silence was that of waiting. It was a silence that seemed poised on the brink of evil.

Shevlin went to his horse and gathered the reins. Yet he hesitated, taking stock of the situation. There was Dr. Clagg—he would stay home this night to protect his home and to protect Laine, and he was a good man, a solid man. . . .

Wilson Hoyt? There was no telling about him. But Ben Stowe would be about, and Gentry, and Ray Hollister.

His thoughts kept returning to Evans. He had known the shyster, as had everyone in Rafter. It was well known that he had a hand in all manner of underhanded things, and he was supposed to have been engaged in smuggling. That didn't make a lot of sense, this far from any border, but it was the gossip. Mason said that Evans had arranged the hiding place for the gold . . . did Mason know that, or was he merely guessing?

Shevlin, his pistol easy in its holster, looked toward the livery stable. He liked that stable—a man could go a lot of directions under cover from there.

He walked down to the street and went across it, taking his own, unhurried time, but his scalp prickled with every step.

The chair beside the stable door was gone, but as he passed under the light and went into the stable, Brazos said, "Shevlin, you sure give a man the willies. You could get yourself killed thataway."

"Maybe."

"Reminds me of a time down Texas way, the night the lid blew off on the Sutton-Taylor feud."

A little wind blew down the street fluttering a bit of white paper. A sign creaked rustily, and in one of the stalls a horse stamped and blew.

Standing in the darkness, just inside the door, Shevlin caught a faint glimmer of light reflected from steel, steel that moved and rattled very faintly. A rider sat his horse in the gap between the buildings.

Swiftly, his eyes went up the street, measuring off the gaps. There could be eight or nine riders waiting there.

Brazos had seen what he had seen, and he spoke quickly. "No miners in town tonight, Mike. Nary a one."

Shevlin absorbed that. Of course. Ben Stowe would hold them, armed and in readiness. There was no longer a light in Stowe's office, nor in the jail office. The only light was the lantern burning over the door.

Mike Shevlin knew enough of Ben Stowe to know he would try to win with one strike, one decisive blow that would cripple the attacking force beyond recovery. He would want a massacre.

It would end the opposition to him, and it would also keep any stories from leaving the town. Prolonged fighting would attract attention; but a quick, sharp fight—one that was soon over—could be brushed off in the local papers as trouble with rustlers or thieves.

Yet there were men on those horses who had once ridden beside Shevlin, good men, honest men, even though they were wrong-headed in this case. He had to stop them.

Ray Hollister would strike at Stowe's office for the records, and at the mines themselves—first the Sun Strike, then the Glory Hole. And Stowe would be waiting, his men armed, no doubt, with shotguns, and hidden all around the collar of the shaft up there, around the mine office, the hoisthouse, and the blacksmith shop. They would be hidden, with protection, and they would be shooting at mounted men outlined against the faint light.

"I'm going across the street," Shevlin said.

"You'll get yourself killed."

"Only," a voice said behind them, "if he tries to leave this stable." It was Babcock.

"Babcock," said Mike, "if you've got any regard for your friends, you'd best get over there and stop them. Stowe's ready for them."

"You mean he *was* ready," Babcock said. "This time we caught him off guard."

"Have you seen any miners around, Babcock? If I was Ray Hollister I'd start looking at my hole card."

"Ray'll take care of himself."

"You bet he will. But where does that leave the rest of you? You've pulled Ray out of more than one mess his fool ideas got you into, so you'd better move fast. If you start up to the mines they'll cut you to doll rags."

"I don't reckon."

Down the street there was a faint shuffle of movement, and Shevlin knew the sound, for he had often heard it at night out on a cattle drive, or when he was bedded near the remuda. Men on horses were moving about.

"You'd better stop them," he said again.

Babcock shifted his feet. "Ease up, now. Nothing and no-body is going to stop Ray this time. You're out of this, Shevlin, so keep out."

"For God's sake, man! Do you really think Ray Hollister is doing this for the cattlemen? Who do you think brought Ben Stowe in in the first place?"

"He brought himself."

"Babcock, don't let loyalty to Hollister kill your friends. You've always been loyal to him, but Ray never thought of anybody but himself. It was the firm of Hollister and Evans who brought Ben Stowe in to head the gunmen who fought the cattle outfits."

"That's a damned lie!" Babcock said hoarsely. "Now you shut your mouth!"

"I don't lie, and you know it. Hollister brought Gentry in, too, along with Ben. You're here tonight, Babcock, to pull the chestnuts out of the fire for Ray. He hopes to get rid of Stowe and get back in the saddle himself."

Babcock's face was set in stubborn lines. There was no arguing with the man, and in not many minutes it would be too late; but Mike Shevlin knew better than to make a wrong move against Babcock now. The cowhand was tough and seasoned, and wily as an old wolf. And that reminded Shevlin of Winkler. Where was the old wolfer, anyway?

The livery stable was dark and still. It was almost as if all were serene. There was the smell of hay and manure, the pleasant smell of horses and a horse barn. The light of the lantern glowed feebly above the door.

It was past two o'clock in the morning; maybe almost three. A good two hours remained before daylight, ample time for whatever mischief was to be done under cover of darkness.

Now in the spaces between the buildings riders could be made out, three abreast in the first opening, two in the next. Others, judging by the sound, were walking their horses slowly up the street.

"Babcock," Shevlin said, "you're sitting in on a wake. Out there in that dusty street you'll see the end of the cattle business in Rafter. You're a stubborn man, and you've been loyal for a long time to a shadow; but stop and think, man.

"You were at Rock Springs the night I whipped Ray. You know Ray never saw the time when he could stand with the big cattlemen in the old days, but he's got Eve Bancroft convinced now that he was a big man. Babcock, be honest . . . did you ever know anybody who was afraid of Ray Hollister?"

"That don't cut no ice."

"You two worked together for a long time," Mike went on, looking hard at Babcock, "but if you'd admit it to yourself, you were the one who built that outfit of his while Ray played the big man. You did the work, managed the place, hired and fired most of the time."

Babcock made no reply. Shevlin looked along the street again. It was not over two hundred yards from here to the mine buildings, but from the moment the men passed the livery stable they would be in at least partial light for the rest of the distance. Anyone who passed this point in full view was a dead man.

"Bab, is Joe Holiday out there?"

"What if he is?"

"I recall a time when Joe pulled a crazy steer off you . . . saved your bacon. You going to let Joe get killed?"

Babcock shifted his feet.

"Bab, you're a good Injun when it comes to scouting. There was a time you'd never have walked into this with your eyes shut. You'd have scouted the lay-out before you made a move."

Shevlin was sure he had Babcock worried, and he pressed the advantage. "Bab, you can make fifty dollars mighty easy. I've got it here, and I'll lay it two to one you'll find fifty, maybe a hundred armed men up at the head of that street."

"You're bluffin'."

"Call me."

Brazos spoke for the first time. "You call him, Babcock, and I'll lay you another fifty you made you a bad bet. They're up there all right."

"Hell," Babcock said, "I couldn't stop them! Ray's got 'em itching for it. The way they feel they'd charge hell with a bucket of water."

The riders were coming on now, a solid rank of them, wall to wall on the street, walking their horses. And as they drew nearer, the rider waiting between the buildings started to move out to join them.

"*Look!*" exclaimed Brazos.

The silent cavalcade had stopped abruptly, almost opposite the livery stable.

A blocky, powerful figure had stepped from the restaurant, a toothpick between his teeth. He stood now in the center of the street—dark, silent, but somehow indomitable.

It was Wilson Hoyt.

TEN

Hoyt wore two six-shooters, and a third was thrust into his waistband. In his hands was a Colt revolving shotgun.

He said not a word. He just stood there, letting them see him, letting them count the odds for themselves. Every man there knew they could ride him down: the question was, who was to die in the process? How many shots could he get off before he went down?

The range was point-blank, and just enough to get a fair spread on his shot; they would be slugs, heavy enough to kill a man. If he could get off two shots he could empty three to six saddles at that range; and he might get out of the way and keep shooting.

Mike Shevlin, watching from the darkness, knew how they felt. Of the forty or so men out there, only two or three might die, *but which ones?*

Wilson Hoyt spoke suddenly, quietly, and he showed his shrewdness in not even glancing toward Ray Hollister. Hollister was the sort that would feel he had to prove himself, no matter who got killed; so Hoyt deliberately threw the responsibility to another.

"Walt Kelly," he said, "you turn this outfit around and ride back where you came from."

"Get out of the way, Hoyt!"

"Don't be a damn' fool, Walt," Hoyt replied in a reasonable tone. "You know this is my job. Did you ever hear of me quitting on the job?"

Mike Shevlin stepped out from the stable. "Back up, boys. That crowd up the street are waiting there in the dark, just praying for you to ride up."

Eyes had turned toward him. Some of them were hard,

hating eyes, some questioning, some even hopeful. In any such crowd there are always a few who do not want the thing to happen, who are wishing for something, anything, to stop it before it goes too far. These found their hope in Hoyt, and now in Shevlin's backing of Hoyt.

But Ray Hollister had been ignored too long. "He's a damn' liar!" he yelled. "There's nobody up there! Come on, let's go!"

There was a noticeable surge in the crowd, and Hoyt's shotgun lifted. "If any of you boys are friendly to Walt Kelly," he said, "you'd better tell him goodbye . . . and there's a couple more had better say it for themselves."

Hoyt had made his mistake. As a crowd, they could hold back and acquire no blame, but now he had named an individual, and one of the best among them. Walt Kelly could not hold back now.

"Damn you, Hoyt!" he said. "Get out of the way. I'm riding!"

"What about Arch, Walt?" Shevlin's voice carried easily.

All his life Walt Kelly had been father as well as big brother to Archer Kelly. And it was Arch's name that made him hesitate now.

At that instant a rider thrust forward from the crowd. It was Eve Bancroft, and her face was white with fury. "You yellow-livered coyotes!" Her voice was hoarse with anger. "Come on, Ray! We'll show 'em!"

She slapped the spurs to her horse and he leaped forward. Hoyt sprang to grab her bridle, but she was past him and charging up the street.

Ray Hollister made one lunge to follow, then pulled up.

Eve Bancroft, her gun blazing, went up the street, and the waiting miners could not see she was a woman. She rode full-tilt into a ripping wall of lead that struck her from the saddle, tearing with hot metal claws at her flesh. She half-turned before she fell clear, and the scream that tore from her throat, a scream of agony and despair, echoed in the street.

From the darkness where the miners lay, a voice called out in horror. "It's a woman! My God, we've killed a woman!"

The eyes of the cattlemen looked at the still figure lying in the street a hundred yards away. And then as one man they looked at Ray Hollister.

Every man of them knew that Eve Bancroft had ridden up the street because she believed in Hollister, and she had invited him to ride with her.

He sat his horse, staring at her body as if he couldn't believe it, scarcely aware as the riders one by one turned and rode away. He had brought her to this, and in the moment of need, he had failed her. He had let her ride alone.

Hoyt moved suddenly. "Hollister, get out of here. If I ever see you again I'll shoot you like a mad dog. I'll kill you where you stand."

People, mysteriously absent until now, began to appear on the street. Two of the women went to Eve's body. Nobody needed to ask if she was dead, for no one could have ridden into that burst of fire and survived.

Shevlin moved up beside Hoyt. "I tried to stop her!" Hoyt said. "Damn it, I tried!"

"Nobody could have stopped her then," Shevlin said. "Nobody but Ray."

People were gathering in clusters on the street, talking. Ben Stowe was nowhere in sight.

"He didn't do a damn' thing," Hoyt said. "He just sat there and watched her go."

"He started," somebody said. "He started, and then he quit . . . he quit cold."

Mike Shevlin turned away, but Hoyt stopped him. "Do you think this will end it?"

"Has anything changed?" Shevlin asked. "A girl's dead that should be alive, but the situation's the same. Hoyt, you take it from me. Throw Ben Stowe in jail. Then call a meeting of half a dozen of your best citizens and get this thing cleaned up."

Hoyt hesitated, staring gloomily before him. "Arrest Ben Stowe? He hired me."

"Hired you to do a job."

Shevlin walked off. He was going back to the claim. Tomorrow was another day, and he had a job to do; and what better place to do some thinking than there with a shovel in his hands?

Suddenly he thought of Burt Parry. Where was he? He had left the claim for town, but Shevlin had seen nothing of him . . . and the town was not that big, not unless he had a girl and was staying with her.

But Shevlin realized that he himself wanted no more of the town, or its people. He had not liked Eve Bancroft, but she had been young and alive, and she had believed in her chosen man. To waste such a faith . . . that was the sad thing, and he had no stomach for what had happened.

All he wanted now was to ride away to where the mountains reached for the sky, where the pines brushed at the clouds. He paused by the stable, and his thoughts were gloomy. He was an old lobo who ran the hills alone, and he had best get used to the idea. There was no use looking into the eyes of any girl. He was the sort who would wind up in the dead end of a canyon, snarling and snapping at his own wounds because of the weakness they brought.

There was nothing here he wanted, nothing but for that old man up on the hillside to rest easy, not buried as a man who died in a gunfight, but as one shot down with empty, innocent hands. For old Eli had never been a man of violence, just as Mike himself was his opposite, a man who walked hard-shouldered at the world.

He got the black horse from the stable and rode him out of town. He avoided the trails, scouting wide upon the grassy hills, and riding the slopes away from the tracks left by horses and men.

When he came to the canyon he had to take the trail, and it was then his horse shied. He drew up, trusting his horse. He sat the saddle silently, listening to the night. At first he heard no sound, and then only a brushing whisper, as of a horse walking past brush that touched his saddle as he went by.

Mike Shevlin stayed still and waited. He was anxious to be back at the claim, and he was irritated at this interruption. There was a faint gray in the far sky, hinting at the dawn that would come soon.

Then he saw the horse, a horse with an empty saddle, head up, looking toward him. The horse whinnied, and his own replied. Coldly, he still waited, his Winchester up and ready for a quick shot.

Nothing happened. . . .

He walked his horse nearer, and saw the white line of the trail, and something dark that lay sprawled there. Shevlin had seen many such dark sprawlings in the night, and he knew what lay there. He stepped down from the saddle, for his horse warned him of no other danger.

He knelt and turned the man over on his back. Then he struck a match, and looked into the wide-open dead eyes of Gib Gentry.

Shevlin struck another match. The front of Gib's shirt, where the bullet had emerged, was dark with blood, almost dry now. In the flare of the match he saw something else.

Gib had crawled after he had fallen. He had crawled four or five feet, and one hand was outstretched toward a patch of brush.

Striking yet another match, Shevlin looked at that outstretched hand and saw, drawn shakily in the sand under the edge of the brush: *Shev look out. Lon C——*

The last word trailed off into a meaningless scrawl.

Shevlin straightened up and looked around. Even in the few minutes since he had first seen the horse, it had grown faintly light, and the country around was slowly defining itself. The half-hour before daybreak brought out a pale gray world with dark patches of brush. Only one or two late stars showed in the sky.

Leaving his own horse, he walked to Gentry's mount. There was blood on the saddle, blood down one side of the skirt. Walking still further back, Shevlin saw where the horse had shied at the bullet, and there he found a spot or two of blood. Gentry had come no more than a dozen yards before toppling from the saddle.

Mike Shevlin pushed his hat back and lifted his face to the fresh coolness of the morning breeze. He looked about him.

There were no other tracks. The hidden marksman had been sure of his shot, or else he had not dared to risk a closer approach to make certain of a kill.

Gib Gentry was dead—but how did that fit into the larger picture? Gentry had been Stowe's strong right hand. Why should he be killed? Gentry had owned the express and freight line, and was necessary to any movement of gold. Looked at coldly, his death was inopportune. The time for it was not now.

Shevlin did not trust Stowe, and he was sure that Stowe would kill any man with whom he had to share as soon as that man was no longer necessary. But as Shevlin saw it, Gentry was necessary. . . . And why kill him *here?*

He might have been followed from town, and if he had been killed intentionally, he obviously had been followed. But this was not a place where Gentry would normally come, so far as Shevlin knew.

So what was the alternative? Gentry must have been killed by mistake. Shot in the dark, mistaken for someone else.

What someone? The answer was plain. For Mike Shevlin himself.

That also made sense of Gentry's message. Gib had been riding to warn him, and he had been mistaken for Shevlin and killed.

Lon C—— . . . Shevlin knew no such name. Yet Gib had evidently thought the name would mean something to him, or he would not have tried so hard to write it.

With the toe of his boot, Shevlin erased the name written in the sand. Then he hoisted Gib's body to the saddle, tied it there, and hung the bridle reins over the pommel. Gentry's horse would go home.

All was dark and silent when he rode up to the claim. He stripped the rig from his horse and picketed it on a grassy slope near the spring, where it could drink from the run-off. He waited in the darkness, listening. After a while he walked back to the cabin and turned in.

He awakened with the sun shining in his eyes through the open door. Burt Parry was standing outside, looking up the canyon, a peculiar expression on his face. For some reason that expression surprised Mike Shevlin.

At that instant Parry seemed anything but the casual man he had been before. He was holding his Winchester in a position to throw it to his shoulder for a quick shot.

Unable to restrain his curiosity, Shevlin swung his feet to the floor. The bunk creaked and Parry looked around quickly.

"Thought I saw a deer," Parry said, lowering the rifle. "We could use some venison."

"Now that's an idea!" Shevlin exclaimed. "How about me going for a hunt?"

Parry chuckled. "You tired of mucking already? I'll have another round of shots ready to fire almost any time." He took Shevlin's appearance in at a glance. "You look like you could use some sleep. What time did you get in?"

"Daybreak, or thereabouts."

He expected a comment on the happenings in town, but none came. He volunteered nothing, and the two men ate breakfast, talking idly of the mining claim and Parry's plans for doing some exploration work in an effort to find the lode he hoped would lie deeper in the mountain.

There was only one explanation for Parry's lack of interest: he simply did not know what had happened in town. And that meant he had not been in Rafter at all.

Where, then, had he been?

ELEVEN

Deliberately, Mike Shevlin offered no comment on the happenings in Rafter, and Burt Parry asked no questions. But Mike knew that the town and all the country around must be talking with excitement about the killing of Eve Bancroft.

The killing of a girl in a western town was itself enough to start such talk, but Eve Bancroft was owner of the Three Sevens. It was not the largest ranch in that region, but it was one of the big ones.

As he worked, Mike Shevlin tried to find a way through this situation, but there seemed to be none. He had attempted to stir up the hornet's nest, but the cattlemen and Ray Hollister had done more than he ever could have. Yet nothing in the situation had changed.

A girl was dead. Ray Hollister was disgraced. Eve Bancroft had called upon him to back his words with action and he had welshed. He had hung back, and Eve had ridden to her death.

What they might have done had Hoyt not been there, Shevlin could not guess. Hoyt could stop them, as he never could have stopped Eve, for to lift his hand against a girl, a decent girl, was unthinkable to a man of Hoyt's stripe. And Ben Stowe, solid, unshaken, still sat his throne in the center of the community.

Shevlin's thoughts returned to Gib Gentry. Without a doubt, Gib had been riding to warn him when he was killed, and without a doubt he had been killed by mistake for Shevlin. Somebody had been lying in wait, and by now that somebody knew he had killed the wrong man.

Each time Shevlin wheeled a load to the end of the dump, he took his time to breathe in plenty of the fresh air, and to look around. It was very quiet. Parry had gone off again, and

Mike was alone at the claim, but there was work enough to keep him busy until midafternoon, barring the unexpected.

He wondered what effect Eve's death would have on the people of Rafter. They were not all bad—in fact, they were no worse than most people in most towns. Perhaps a few more had been willing to go along than would usually be found, but there must have been some dissenting opinions, even though the people who held those opinions had kept still.

Such fear as he had seen in Rafter could not continue very long. The people were wary, they doubted every stranger; they lived with the worry that at any moment the house they had built would come tumbling about their ears.

He was working close against the face of the drift, scraping up the last of the rock, when it came to him.

Lon Court . . .

Of course. He *had* heard the name. Gentry had scratched *Lon C* into the sand before he died, and Shevlin remembered that he had once heard talk of Lon Court, a killer, a man who worked for big cattle outfits, or anyone else who had need of his services. A mysterious, solitary man who could be hired to kill. He was just such a man as Ben Stowe would have hired.

Undoubtedly Court had scouted the mining claim. He might even now be lying up on the lip of the canyon across from the tunnel mouth, and with every barrow of rock Shevlin had wheeled out he had been a sitting duck.

There was no longer any hesitation in Mike Shevlin, for he knew now what he must do. He must get out of the tunnel and get to his guns, and he must get out of the canyon, which was a death trap with a man like Court stalking him. And then he must find Court and kill him.

There was no alternative, no other way possible, for Court would never quit once he had undertaken a job. He, Mike Shevlin, must hunt the hunter, stalk the killer, and he must kill him.

He put down his shovel. The last barrow could stand where it was. There was, of course, a chance that Lon Court was not waiting on the hill opposite; he certainly would not be unless there was an easy escape from it. Trust a killer like Lon Court to take no unnecessary risk.

Shevlin went as far along the tunnel as he could without getting into the sunlight, and then he squatted down and peered out, keeping well in the shadow. By squatting, he could see the rim without going further. He stayed there and studied it for a long time.

No brush grew on the rim, and there were no boulders, no

spot where water had cut into the rim and made a place where a man might lie concealed. Flattening himself tight to the wall, Shevlin worked his way to the tunnel mouth. Then he emerged quickly and went toward the cabin, making three sudden turns for objects in his path, turns sufficient to make timing his movements awkward for anyone watching. Once inside the cabin, he stripped off his shirt, washed his chest and shoulders, then combed his hair, and belted on his gun. He thrust a second six-shooter into his waistband and took up his rifle.

The black horse was picketed on the grass near the spring, but the killer must descend into the canyon to get a good shot at him there. Mike Shevlin did not think Lon Court would take such a gamble.

He went to his horse, took the saddle from a shelf in the rock close by, and saddled up. The horse tugged toward the run-off stream, so while he let the gelding drink, Shevlin listened.

That canyon worried him, and he recalled the sudden cessation of sound from the birds that he had noticed. Something— and he was sure it had been a man—had walked up that canyon in the late afternoon.

Leaving the black with trailing reins, he went down to the bottom of the canyon and worked his way across it. Here and there were the tracks of small animals . . . a porcupine or badger whose tracks were somewhat smudged . . . many quail tracks . . . the tracks of a prowling coyotes . . . and on the far side where a dim trail wound under the rim, the smudged tracks of a tall man's boots.

So someone *had* gone up the canyon. The tracks were a day or two old; but searching further, he found other, more recent ones.

He had turned to go back to his horse when he happened to look down the canyon. Standing on the old dump—the place Parry had said was the discovery claim of the Sun Strike—was Parry himself. He held a rifle, and he was staring down the canyon toward the claim.

Gathering the bridle reins, Shevlin started along the path from the spring to the claim. He watched Burt without turning his head toward him, striving to appear unaware of the other man's presence.

Suddenly, Parry heard him, and turned sharply. He held his rifle ready, and Shevlin was himself poised to drop to one knee and fire, if it came to that. He had no idea why Parry might decide to shoot, but the other man's oddly secretive manner made him wary.

Parry spoke. "I was looking for you. Did you finish up at the claim?"

"Sure . . . all but the last wheelbarrow. I just played out, figured to go in after it later. You been in town?"

Parry's eyes searched his. "There was hell to pay. Why didn't you tell me?"

"Well, I knew Eve. She offered me a job, you know, and I was kind of upset over it. Just didn't feel like talking about it. Besides, I figured you knew."

They walked back to the claim. Burt Parry's open, casual manner returned. "Too bad," he said; "she was a pretty girl."

Mike Shevlin paused. "Burt," he said, "have you ever been in a western town when a good woman got killed?"

"No . . . why?"

"You've got something to learn. Even when any kind of a woman is killed or hurt, I've seen a town go wild. Believe me, there's a lot of talking and thinking, and checking of hole cards going on in that town and in all the Rafter country right now. This ain't over—not by a long shot."

Parry's brow furrowed, but then he shrugged. "Hell, I'm out of it. I've never mixed in their squabbles."

"That won't cut any ice. Vigilantes have a way of lynching the wrong folks. You ever hear of Jack Slade? He got drunk on the wrong night and raised a lot of hell, so when they started lynching the Plummer gang they just hung him, too, on general principles."

Parry scowled, and rubbed his jaw. They paused at the cabin. "You riding in?"

"Uh-huh." Mike let his eyes scan the rim with a swift but careful glance. "And I may just scout me a quick way out of this country. I might decide to tuck in my tail and run."

He had no such intention, but he trusted no one any longer, and it was just as well to keep his plans to himself. And he had several things to do that might keep him out of town.

Rafter Crossing lay in a shallow valley, with the Sun Strike Mine occupying a bench south of the town; further back and somewhat higher was the Glory Hole. The ridges were timbered, except for the one where the mines were located, but in the low country there were no trees except along the infrequent water courses. Here were cottonwoods or low-growing willows.

Mike Shevlin had punched cows over this country for several years, which was to say that he knew it intimately. When a cowhand hunts strays, gathering stock for a roundup or a cattle drive, he works every draw, every canyon. Soon there's not an inch of the country he hasn't seen, or that hasn't been described in detail by other cowhands. But today Mike Shevlin was not hunting strays, he was hunting a man.

Hiding out in wild country is not as simple as it may seem, for a man must be in the proximity of water. And for a man who does not wish to be seen, that means a water hole that is off the line of travel, and out of the area covered by drifters or cowhands working the range. Such a man must have not only water, he must have freedom from observation, easy access to and from his hide-out, and especially a good field of observation to watch anyone who might be approaching.

Such places were few in this region. The need for water limited them drastically, for water was scarce, and most places where it could be found had been settled on. There were only a few other places that remained, and Mike Shevlin believed he knew them all. As he rode he took them one by one and examined them with care, and when he had ridden six miles he had eliminated all but one.

Boulder Spring was not as remote as such places usually are; it was only off the beaten track. Moreover, in that particular area, water was not scarce. Anyone riding to Boulder Spring from any one of three directions must cross a small stream, and in the fourth direction there was a good water hole. It was the perfect hide-out, and there was no reason for anyone to go there at all.

It lay several miles off the travel routes in a huddle of low ridges and hills, a patch of heaped-up, sunburned boulders, browned by time and the wind and sun. Around them lay an acre or so that was flat sand grown up with a little mesquite, a little *cholla*, and some cat-claw. On the ridges juniper grew.

In among the rocks, and not easily found, was a cold spring of very good water. Wind blew through the rocks and over the spring, so the air right at the water was always cool, and often cold.

In under the boulders were several low caves where a man might bed down, and each of them had more than one approach. On low ground nearby, in the open but actually difficult to see, were places where a man might leave a couple of horses.

Most of the Rafter range that lay in this direction had been abandoned since the mines started up and old Jack was killed, and few riders would be rustling around near Boulder Spring.

Though Lon Court might have holed up at any of the other spots, Mike Shevlin was gambling that Boulder Spring was the place.

Next he reviewed the little he knew of Lon Court. The man was not a gunfighter—he was a killer. He hunted men the way old Winkler hunted wolves; he stalked them, and killed them when he could do so safely. That did not imply the man was a physical coward, and Shevlin was sure he was not. To Lon Court killing was a business, and he took no chances on being wounded or being seen by his victims or by anyone else. The very nature of his calling depended on being unknown.

To secure his own safety, Mike Shevlin knew he must find Lon Court before the killer found him, but there was little time, for he must also find the gold.

He was sure that Gib Gentry had been deliberately set up in the freighting business so the gold could be shipped with maximum security and a minimum of talk, and now that Gentry was out of the picture, who would take over? Who would handle the shipment? And might they not direct every effort toward getting the gold out of the country while they could?

He had tried to stir things up so that Ben Stowe would be forced to make a move, yet now Stowe might settle right back and wait, for he was a canny man, and not one to be hurried.

Suddenly, the horse's ears came up sharply. Shevlin slowed his pace a little, searching the country.

He stopped none too soon, for even as his own mount became motionless, a rider emerged from a draw about two hundred yards off. He was a tall man riding a long-legged *grulla*, a tough, mouse-colored mountain horse. The man wore a narrow-brimmed hat and a nondescript gray coat. And he was following a trail.

Shevlin's position was excellent. His horse had come to a dead stop, half sheltered by boulders, stunted juniper, and low brush. He spoke softly to his horse, and sat his saddle, waiting.

The man held a rifle in his right hand, and he rode slowly, checking the trail from time to time. He was surely following someone, following with great care, and it was Shevlin's guess that the man's quarry was not far ahead of him. And at the same instant Mike Shevlin realized with startling clarity that this was Lon Court.

He was as positive of it as if the man had been identified by a pointing finger. Everything about him fitted the picture Shevlin had made from bits he recalled hearing; coupled with this was the man's presence here, and his manner.

Mike Shevlin slid his rifle from its scabbard and let the rider take a little more lead.

Then he started his own horse down the trail after him.

TWELVE

He left the trail to his horse, hardly daring to shift his attention from the man ahead of him for a moment. He would get only one chance if Lon Court saw him, for the man would shoot—instantly, and with accuracy.

Who was the man following? Obviously it was someone only a short distance ahead, or he would be riding with greater speed. He was keeping his eyes on the trail left by the rider, and he too was taking no chances.

The man's horse, the nondescript clothing—neither of them stood out. He merged into the background of desert and boulders, so that at a greater distance than he was from Shevlin he would have been scarcely visible.

The day was warm. Sweat trickled down Mike Shevlin's neck, beaded on his forehead. He shifted his hands on the Winchester and dried his palms on his shirt front. By now Court was slanting up the hill, as if about to top out on the crest.

Court dismounted and, rifle in hand, moved to the top of the ridge. He was easing his rifle to his shoulder when suddenly he seemed to freeze, his attention riveted on something beyond the ridge.

Mike Shevlin's horse was in sand now, walking carefully and making no sound, and Shevlin was closing the distance between them, drawing steadily nearer the sniper on the ridge.

When still perhaps sixty yards off, Shevlin drew up and dismounted, trailing his reins. He desperately wanted to know what lay beyond that ridge, to see who it was that Court was stalking, but there was no possibility of that.

Lon Court was as dangerous as a cornered rattler, and never so dangerous as he would be now, if caught in the act. Only his concentration on his job had permitted Shevlin to come so close as this.

The warm air was still. The only sound was a cicada singing in the brush near the road. Shevlin, careful not to start a stone rolling to warn Court, worked his way silently along the slope. Then he paused and, choosing two small pebbles from the gravel near his feet, he flipped one at Court's horse. The *grulla* jumped and snorted.

Lon Court whipped around as quick as a cat, looking toward the horse.

"Over here, Lon!"

Lon Court wheeled and fired in the same instant, but he fired too soon. His bullet was a little high, but Mike Shevlin's was more carefully aimed. Pointed for the middle of Court's chest, it struck the hammer on the rifle and deflected upward, ripping Court's throat and jaw.

Desperately, Court tried to work his rifle, then he dropped it and grabbed for his six-shooter. He was on his feet, standing with them slightly apart, the old narrow-brimmed hat pulled down over his eyes. His yellow mustache showed plainly.

Shevlin stepped off to his right and fired again, the bullet turning Court, whose shot went wild. Court brought his gun back on target just as Shevlin fired his third shot, putting it right through Court's skull.

Mike walked up to the dead man and looked down at him. He felt no regret or pity. Lon Court had chosen his path with his eyes open, and must have known that someday it would end just as it had. In his time he had killed a lot of men, and now he lay dead himself, killed by one of those he had been sent to get.

Returning to his horse, Shevlin mounted up and went over the ridge. In the valley beyond there was a dim trail, an old trail. On it he found the tracks of a horse, and followed them.

When he had gone only a few feet he saw where the horse had dug in hard and taken off on a hard run. The rider must have been at that point when he heard the shots.

Shevlin was almost on the edge of town, still following the tracks, before he caught sight of the rider. It was Laine Tennison.

She pulled off to the side of the trail and waited when she saw him coming.

"Scare you?" he asked.

"Was that you back there?"

"Uh-huh. I was one of them."

She looked at him searchingly. "What happened?"

"There was a man named Lon Court. Been around for years.

He hires out to big cattle outfits or anybody who has killing they want done. He was laying for you."

"And you stopped him?"

"Don't make a lot of it. I was on his list, too."

"You . . . you killed him?"

"Ma'am," Shevlin said dryly, "you never get far talking things over with a man holding a gun. And this here man wasn't much given to talk."

"What's going to happen now?"

"As a result of that? Well, when a man like Lon Court dies nobody cares much. Not in this country, in these times.

"As to what will happen, I wouldn't know. We're going to ride into Rafter, you and me, and this time you're going to stay there with the Claggs, and don't leave there or I'll quit the whole thing. I can't be running around looking after you, with everything else I've got to do."

The streets were strangely empty when they came into town. After leaving Laine at the Claggs', Mike Shevlin rode to the sheriff's office.

Wilson Hoyt looked up sourly, and with no welcome. "All right, what's your argument?"

"I just came in to report a shooting. Lon Court is dead."

Hoyt knew the name. He turned the idea over in his mind, growing angrier by the minute. "Who the hell brought him in here?" he said.

"Somebody who wanted Laine Tennison killed. Somebody who wanted me killed, and who killed Gib Gentry by mistake."

"You think Court killed Gentry?"

"The only man who was supposed to be riding that trail that night was me," Shevlin said. "Only Gentry was coming to see me—to warn me, in fact."

Wilson Hoyt considered this. He put it together with a few other facts. Gib Gentry had been drinking the night before he was killed, but that was not unusual, for Gib had been hitting the bottle a lot these last few months.

Hoyt had, in his slow, methodical, yet thorough way traced Gentry's movements. Nobody had anything to conceal and they trusted Hoyt, as they had, for the most part, liked Gentry. Gentry had been a rough-and-ready but free-handed man who made no enemies. The last man who had spoken to Gentry was Brazos, when Gib got his horse, and Gib had definitely been riding after Shevlin.

What disturbed Hoyt was the knowledge that just before Gentry went to the stable for his horse he had a brief talk with

Red, and then Red had ridden off out of town. Shortly after, Gentry had gone for his horse.

"Lon Court hadn't been in town," Hoyt said. "I didn't even know he'd been in the country. If I had, I'd have run him the hell out of it."

"Lon Court never rode a mile without being paid for it," Shevlin said. "Who do you think stands to gain by having me killed? By having Laine Tennison killed?"

"Where does she fit into this?"

"Somebody thinks she might be an owner. Clagg Merriam learned the other night that she had wealthy connections in Frisco. The Sun Strike is owned in Frisco."

"They wouldn't murder a woman."

"You forget mighty quick. What about Eve Bancroft?"

"That was a mistake."

Wilson Hoyt looked up at Shevlin sharply. "Clagg Merriam? What the hell has he got to do with this?"

"He's the man behind Ben Stowe."

Hoyt's little world of certainties was toppling. "Like hell!" he exclaimed. "Mr. Merriam scarcely knows Ben—and he's a respected man."

Mike Shevlin did not feel like arguing with him. He would leave it to Hoyt's solid common sense. He was tired, but there was much to be done.

He leaned over the desk. "Hoyt," he said, "your nice playhouse is ruined for good, and you might as well look at it straight. Maybe you can pull this town out of the hole it's in . . . maybe you can't. I figure most of these folks—even those who've been shutting their eyes to what goes on—are good folks, given a chance.

"But Eve Bancroft is dead, and that's getting to them. They won't stand still for it, the way I see it. All you'd have to do would be to get up and make a stand, and you'd have them behind you. If you don't, your rep as a town pacifier is finished, because there'll be more killings."

"You said Court was dead."

"Do you think he would have to do it all? I know Ben, Hoyt; I've known him a long time. He's a mighty tough man, grown tougher with years, and he plays hard. Believe me, they got Gib by mistake, but I'd lay a bet he was on the list to die . . . after he'd done his job for them."

It made sense, of course. Wilson Hoyt was a man of no illusions, and once he faced the situation he would see the thing straight. Like many another man, he faced the fact of change reluctantly. He had had two good years in Rafter, relatively peaceful years, and although he must have known the situation could not last, he had been willing to go along with it. His own job was to keep the peace, not to be a guardian of morals . . . that was the way he had allowed himself to think.

But now he could no longer stand aside. He had made a move; he had averted the calamity of a street battle between miners and cattlemen—and Eve Bancroft had been killed. He had believed it was over then, but here was Mike Shevlin, assuring him it had only begun.

Lon Court was dead, but that had happened out of town, and was not his concern. The presence of Lon Court was, for somebody within the town had brought him here.

And now Shevlin had brought Clagg Merriam into the picture. Hoyt hated to think Merriam was involved, yet in the back of his mind he must have sensed it all the time. His surprise had been purely vocal . . . within himself he had felt no such surprise. A man could not move around such a small town without knowing a great deal that was not on the surface.

"All right, Mike," Hoyt said at last, "I'll see what I can do."

He looked up with sudden discouragement. "Hell, Mike, what's a man to do? I figured this was my place to roost. I thought I'd dug myself in for life."

"Maybe you have. Look at it this way, Hoyt. You straighten up this mess, straighten out the town, and with no more fuss than necessary, and you may be home. They may want you to stay."

Wilson Hoyt nodded slowly, doubtfully. As Shevlin walked out, Hoyt stared bleakly across the street at nothing at all.

Ben Stowe pushed the heavy ledgers away from him and pulled open the drawer where he kept his cigars. He selected one, bit off the end, and lit up. Then he sat back and put his feet up on his desk, inhaling deeply. He exhaled the smoke slowly and stared out of the window toward the mountains.

Clagg Merriam was right. They would have to ship some gold. Their working capital was finished. Without cash from somewhere, they could buy up no more gold; and when they stopped buying they would lose control, once and for all. When gold was shipped from the town through business channels, questions would be asked, men would come flooding in.

The deals for the mines must be closed at once, but there

had been no response from San Francisco since his last offer.
Were they investigating? And if so, who?

Clagg Merriam, he knew, was worried about Laine Tennison,
the pretty girl over at the Doc's place. . . . Well, Lon Court
would take care of that.

Ben Stowe scowled with irritation. That damned Gentry! He
would have to go riding out just when Court was expecting
Mike Shevlin. Ben was not in the least disturbed by Gentry's
death, for the time had been appointed . . . but he had needed
him to handle the gold shipment first.

With Gib Gentry dead, all his nicely arranged setup was
spoiled. Moreover, who did he know who could be trusted
with that much gold? Above all, trusted not to talk, and trusted
not to let it be taken away from him?

He could handle it himself, but the town needed a tight rein
right now, and he dared not be away. And most important, the
offer might come from the mine owners, and he must act
promptly.

Who, then, could he get?

Wilson Hoyt would be perfect, but Hoyt had been acting
strange the past few days, and Ben Stowe hesitated to approach
him. Hoyt, he felt, was an honest man, or he seemed to be,
but he had always been a man who kept his eyes strictly on the
job, and did not worry about anything outside it.

Mike Shevlin . . .

Ridiculous as the idea was, Ben kept coming back to it, for
Mike had the guts to deliver that gold, come hell or high
water; and Mike wouldn't talk. Of all the men he knew, Mike
Shevlin was the best man to handle that gold.

The trouble was, Mike was bucking him.

Ben Stowe glanced at the gathering ash on his cigar. Carefully,
he assayed all he knew of Mike Shevlin. He had been a tough
kid, handy with a gun, and not above driving off a few cows
once in a while. He had balked at outright robbery when the
rest of them went into it; but that, Ben decided, was mostly
because Mike had just wanted to drift—he just wanted to get
out and see more country.

Ben had heard a lot of the conflicting stories about Mike
Shevlin. He had been mixed up in some cattle wars, in some
gunfighting, and he had ridden the side of the law a time or
two. That needn't mean a thing, for Ben knew of several
outlaws who had been town marshals, and good ones.

He had never really liked Mike Shevlin, but this was not the
time for that. Suppose . . . just suppose . . . that he made an
offer? Gib's piece of the action, for instance?

There were not many who could turn their backs on a quarter of a million dollars. Of course, Shevlin would never live to collect, no more than Gib Gentry would have.

What fool would give up money of that kind when he could keep it for himself?

But one other thing worried him. Ray Hollister was still out there, and Hollister had to die.

THIRTEEN

Where was Ray Hollister now? Three men were thinking about that.

Mike Shevlin, riding back to the claim in the canyon, was asking himself that question. Ben Stowe, in his office, was worrying about the same thing; and Wilson Hoyt, turning his mind from his recent words with Shevlin, thought again of Hollister.

Not one of them believed he was through. Mike Shevlin, riding warily, and well off the trail, knew that Ray Hollister would never be able to convince himself he was through in Rafter. The thought of going elsewhere would not occur to him, or if it did, it would be dismissed.

Like many another man, he was committed to the home grounds. He could not bring himself to move, although all the world offered a fresh start—new ranges, new towns, places where he was unknown, and where his abilities might have made a place for him.

Right now Hollister was sitting beside a fire in a remote spot among the bare hills. He was alone except for Babcock, and Babcock was for the first time looking on his boss with some doubt.

Only a part of his doubt was the result of his conversation with Shevlin in the stable. His loyalties were deep-seated, and he hesitated, feeling uncertain for the first time in years.

"Where the hell is Wink?" Hollister said, looking up.

"He'll be along."

Winkler had gone down to the Three Sevens to pick up some grub. They had nothing to eat and he knew the cook there. Winkler would have to be careful, for there would be no friendly feeling for them at the Three Sevens. Nor at any of the other ranches, for that matter.

Ray Hollister looked haggard, his face was drawn, his eyes deep-sunken. "Bab," he said, "they've got to move the gold. And if they try to move it, we can get it."

Babcock straightened his thin frame and went over to the nearby brush to pick up sticks for the fire.

"If we can get that gold," Hollister went on, "we'll have them where the hair's short."

"How'll they move it?" asked Babcock.

"Gentry's freight outfit. That was why he was set up that way."

Babcock had squatted on his heels to pick up the sticks, but now he turned his scrawny neck and looked back at Hollister. "That's good figurin'. How'd you know that?"

"I know plenty."

Babcock came back to the fire and added some of the fuel to it. Then he squatted down beside it.

Ray Hollister had forgotten, for the time being, that Babcock knew nothing of his previous arrangements with Ben Stowe. He was thinking aloud rather than planning; and weariness as well as the defeats of the past days had dulled his senses.

Babcock had room for two loyalties and no more, and he believed them to be one and the same. He was loyal to Hollister, and he was loyal to the cattle business. He had grown up around cattle, had worked cattle since he was a child, and had never considered anything else. The discovery of gold at Rafter was a personal affront. He disliked the miners, disliked the camp followers, and most of all he disliked the dirty machinery and the pound of the compressor. When the mines began using great quantities of water and returning some of it muddy and filthy, he was deeply angered.

He had known of the firm of Hollister and Evans, but he had believed it to be a land and investment operation. He had largely ignored it, for Ray was always going off on some new scheme, but he always came back when the scheme proved to be a swindle or a fool notion. While Ray Hollister took off on his other activities, Babcock was minding the cattle.

After the water was polluted, it had been necessary to drive the cattle back from the stream where they had always watered, something it was not easy to do. The only other water was too far away for the good of the stock, and the grass there was poor. He could have used Hollister's help then, for they were short-handed; several of the newer boys had gone off prospecting . . . as if they knew anything about finding gold!

With the hands that remained Babcock had pushed the cattle back from the water with only a few lost, and there had been a time when he had been up to his ears in work far on the other side of the range. Anyway, Babcock himself had never been much of a hand for raising hell in town.

Now, Babcock's mind had not let go of Ray Hollister's comment on why Gentry had been set up that way. Of course, he thought, it was something a man might guess at, or figure out. He looked across the fire at Hollister, considering him thoughtfully, and remembering what Shevlin had said.

He was a man slow to arrive at any conclusion, and he was taking great care in trying to think this matter out. But as he considered it, little bits and pieces of half-forgotten conversations returned to mind.

"They've got to move it!" Hollister exclaimed again suddenly. "They daren't take a chance on running short of cash, or being caught with the gold." He looked shrewdly at Babcock. "Bab, we could have a piece of money out of this."

"I'm no thief." Babcock spoke irritably, for he did not like to have his thinking interrupted. "That money ain't mine."

"It's not theirs, either," Hollister protested, and then added, more slyly, "Without that money those mines won't operate long."

That made a kind of sense, Babcock agreed. "It would be guarded," he suggested.

Hollister dismissed that with a wave of the hand. "Of course it would. But we'd have surprise on our side, and that counts for a lot." He paused. "We'd need a couple of good men, aside from you and Wink and me."

"There's Halloran . . . and John Sande."

Yes, they were good men. Ray Hollister considered the route the gold would be likely to take. Understanding the problem, as probably nobody else did quite so well, he knew the gold must go east. On the west coast the channels of finance were narrow, and there would be too much chance of talk. California was filled with rumors upon rumors, everybody was agog for discoveries, and the slightest suggestion of gold appearing from a new source would set off a rush. Such an amount of gold as this might be more easily handled if it could be shipped to the East.

One by one he went over the routes in his mind, and one by one he eliminated them until only two were left, and of these one was very doubtful.

Winkler rode in before midnight. He sat down on a rock and listened to Hollister's plan. "All right," he said, "count on me. . . . What about Halloran and Sande?"

"They'll go," Babcock said.

Suspicion was not a normal attitude for Babcock. He was a man who did his job, whatever it was, did it simply and directly, and with no nonsense, nor did he allow any nonsense from anyone else.

The handling of cattle was not only his job, it was his vocation; it was the biggest part of his life, and aside from the problems of cattle, nothing had ever seemed important for any length of time. He was always concerned with range conditions, water supplies, noxious weeds, and the amount of beef that could be packed on a steer's frame.

From the hour of rising, usually before sunup, until dusk or after, he lived, breathed, and thought cattle. If Babcock ever dreamed, it was only of greener pastures, clearer water, and a short drive to market. He had never taken time out to consider Ray Hollister as anything but a boss who permitted him freedom in the job he knew best; but now the ugly thought was growing in him that Hollister might actually have been involved with Ben Stowe.

The arrival of Jess Winkler had interrupted his thoughts. He had a sort of respect for the wolfer, but had never liked him, for, as is often the case, the hunter had taken on some of the qualities of the creature he hunted. Winkler could not approach anything—a strange camp, a house, a person, or an idea—without circling warily and sniffing the breeze from every angle. He was a man with the suspicions of a wolf. He had trapped, so he feared traps.

Winkler had held a rough affection for Eve Bancroft, but he had considered her too notional, too feminine. He did not trust Hollister, and he also did not trust Babcock, nor anybody else he could think of at the present time. He was a hard old man whose rifle was an extension of himself.

It had not yet occurred to him that his stake in the game had gone with the death of Eve Bancroft. The idea of taking gold away from the mining outfit appealed to him, and gave direction to his days, at least for a little while.

Two days later, Halloran and John Sande rode in, and as Babcock had promised, they were ready. Winkler would ride in to town to nose about and see what he could discover. The others, after some discussion, decided upon a rendezvous at Boulder Spring. It was close enough to Rafter, had good grass and water, and yet was out of the way.

All was quiet at Parry's claim cabin when Mike Shevlin returned. But Parry was nowhere to be seen, nor was there any indication that he had been around the place for hours. Mike went back into the mine tunnel, but no further work had been done there.

Suddenly feeling uneasy, he came back to the cabin. The canyon was utterly still . . . unnaturally so.

Seated on a bench outside the cabin door, Mike Shevlin cleaned and oiled his Winchester, and then his pistols, working steadily, but with one of the guns always at hand and in operating order. Carefully, he sorted over in his mind all he knew of Burt Parry, and it was very little.

Where did Burt Parry go when he left the claim, Shevlin wondered. The question had been at the back of his mind, but now for the first time he brought it out into the open to consider.

He certainly had not gone to town, though he had ridden in that direction. Aside from the fact that he had disclaimed any interest in the difficulties of the people around Rafter, and had even disclaimed any interest in the gold or the high-grading, he had said very little. However, one thing stuck in Shevlin's mind. The first time he had seen Parry in the café, he had been in conversation with Clagg Merriam.

That in itself need not mean anything at all. Parry seemed a man of some education, appeared to be of eastern background, and he might have some things in common with Merriam.

Shevlin glanced up the canyon now, his eyes resting on the dump at the mouth of the old tunnel—the discovery claim, Parry had said.

Coming back to his mind was Hoyt's comment that the high-grade lay between the two mines, and that at the first hint of discovery the approach tunnels would be blasted shut. Those explosives should be found and removed, but that was not up to him. First, he must find the cache of gold bullion.

Feeling restless, he wandered back into Parry's tunnel, considering the idea of drilling a round of holes. He scanned the walls, and realized for the first time that the rock showed no evidence of minerals, no quartz, nothing at all but ordinary rock.

Returning to the outside, he backed off to the edge of the bench and studied the slope above the mine. He saw no promising outcropping, nor any sign of work; yet Parry's ore was supposed to have been located by a find somewhere on that slope.

Suppose there was no ore there? Suppose this operation, this mining claim of Parry's, was a fake, a blind, just a useful cover for some other operation? What, then, would it be? An investigator of some kind? It was possible. Or . . . suppose

Parry was put here to watch something? Suppose during those mysterious absences he was keeping guard over something?

Mike Shevlin sat down on the bench and lit a cigar. Suppose, then . . . suppose just for the sake of argument that Burt Parry was guarding the gold itself. Was he guarding it for the combine? Or for one of them against the others?

Stifling his excitement, Shevlin began to consider this new possibility. Actually, it was of no importance to him just why Parry was watching the gold, if that was what he was doing. What was important was the obvious fact that if he was watching the gold it must be close by. The mining claim must have been located just where it was for a reason.

Parry always went down the canyon, but did he continue in that direction? Or did he return under cover of the brush in the canyon bottom?

Shevlin had once seen him standing on the dump at the mouth of the old discovery tunnel.

The old discovery tunnel! He got up, his mouth suddenly dry. Suppose . . . ?

He turned away sharply, and picked up his rifle No use saddling his horse. The tunnel was only a few minutes walk up the canyon.

He had not reached the spring when he heard a clatter of horse's hoofs on the trail from Rafter. He hesitated, swore softly, then turned around, and retraced his steps.

As he got to the cabin, the rider came into the open area on the bench. It was Red . . . the miner with whom he had had trouble the day he arrived in Rafter.

"Get your horse," Red said abruptly. "Ben Stowe wants to see you!"

Mike Shevlin looked at him calmly, then took the stub of the extinguished cigar from his pocket and put it between his teeth. He struck a match with his left hand and lifted it to light the cigar.

"If Ben Stowe wants to see me, he knows where to find me."

Red looked surprised. "You want me to tell him *that?*"

"You tell him whatever you've a mind to."

Red stared at him. "I got a damn' good notion to take you in," he said.

"All right," Shevlin replied, "go ahead. You take me!"

FOURTEEN

Red hesitated a moment, then backed down. "The hell with it! If you don't want to come, that's your hard luck. I'll tell Ben."

He wheeled his horse and started away, muttering to himself. From the top of a rise in the narrow trail he glanced back. Mike Shevlin was gone. "Now where the devil—?"

Red drew rein and turned in his saddle. Where could Shevlin have gone so suddenly? As far as that went, where had he been coming from when he rode up? He had acted surprised, and he had seemed hurried.

Red pulled his horse over against the rock wall where they would be less visible, and he watched the canyon for some time. Then he saw a figure appear on the dump of the old discovery claim. It was Mike Shevlin, and he vanished into the tunnel.

When several minutes passed and he did not emerge, Red swung his horse and cantered off toward town.

All was quiet when he rode up the street. Hoyt was standing in front of his office, and Doc Clagg was walking along with his sister and that Tennison girl who was visiting them.

The door of Ben Stowe's office was locked, so Red went across to the Nevada House, where he found Stowe eating.

"He wouldn't come," Red said. "He said if you wanted to see him, you knew where he was."

Surprisingly enough, Ben Stowe did not seem angered at that. "All right," he said mildly. "I'll ride out that way."

"You won't find him," Red said. "He's prowling around up the canyon. I saw him going into the old discovery tunnel."

Ben Stowe's features stiffened, and the hand that held the fork gripped hard. But when he spoke, his voice was casual.

"How long ago was that?"

"Long as it took me to ride in. I came right along."

"Thanks, Red. You hang around town, d'you hear? I might need you."

When Red had gone, Ben Stowe put his fork down slowly. His appetite was gone completely. He had been a fool to allow Shevlin to go to work up there, but Clagg Merriam had said there was nothing to worry about. Working for Burt Parry would keep him out of trouble, and nobody ever saw anything that was right under their nose, anyway. It had seemed a good idea at the time. Maybe it was still a good idea.

He had planned to offer Shevlin the place Gentry had held; now he was not so sure. It was unlikely that Shevlin would find anything; and if he did, they might still make a deal. But why was Shevlin nosing around? What was he looking for? And where was Burt Parry?

It would not do to move hastily, and above all, Red's suspicions must not be aroused. Of course, he had told Red he would ride out and talk to Shevlin, and so he would. There are some things a man had better do himself.

He forced himself to eat a little more, and to take his time over another cup of coffee.

What he did within the next few hours could mean the difference between success and failure, between wealth and poverty, even between life and death.

For the first time in his life he felt haunted by uncertainties. His life until this minute had been relatively simple, but within a matter of days, hours even, the certainties had vanished.

With Gib Gentry's death, the keystone of his plan was gone. He had come to despise Gentry, but the man had been essential to their plan, with the freighting company carefully set up for the purpose. His death, through Lon Court's mistake, left a gaping hole in the carefully planned structure.

And that girl at Doc Clagg's—who was she? What was she?

Irritation mounted within him, an irritation that was born of panic, a panic he stifled. There was no reason to get stirred up. First, he must find Mike Shevlin, find out how much he knew, and whether or not he would go along with Ben Stowe.

Thinking of Shevlin's suggestion that Stowe ride out of town to see him, he swore bitterly, hating the idea of approaching Shevlin with a proposition. Unfortunately, he knew of nobody else who might get that gold safely to its destination, nobody at all.

He had an uneasy feeling that things were getting out of

hand, yet, despite the unfortunate killing of Eve Bancroft, nothing really seemed amiss that couldn't be taken care of.

Ray Hollister was out of it . . . he was finished. Ben Stowe should have been pleased about that, but Hollister had been a gathering point for his enemies. As long as Hollister was around, Stowe had always known where the cattlemen would be.

He went now to the livery stable, strolling casually along the street. He wanted his manner to be remembered: he was a man going for a little ride after lunch, something he had done occasionally over the years. That he was going to win an ally or kill a man before the day was over was something nobody must guess.

Brazos was not at the stable. Ben Stowe had grown accustomed to service, and he disliked saddling his own horse. Irritably, he saddled up, led the horse outside, and stepped into the saddle. Where was that damned hostler, anyway?

At that very moment Brazos was seated in the kitchen of Dr. Clagg's home with a shotgun across his knees, and close at hand, a Winchester .44. He had been recruited by Clagg as a guard for Laine Tennison.

In Clagg's office several patients had arrived for consultation. Billy Townsend, owner of the Blue Horn Saloon, James Martin Field, editor and publisher of the *Rafter Blade,* and Tom Hayes, who operated a general store, were all there. There were several others, chosen with care.

Clagg was speaking to them.

"We will waste no time arguing about the past. What remains is to see what possibilities are open to us now. If any of you have any doubts as to the purpose of our meeting, it is just this: to consider the state of affairs in Rafter as of this minute.

"A young woman, a well-known and generally respected owner of a ranch, has been shot down on the streets of Rafter. Gib Gentry, a businessman of this town, has been murdered just outside it. A notorious killer, imported for what reason we do not know, has been slain in the hills nearby. These killings have all happened in the last few days."

Hayes shifted uncomfortably, and sweat began to bead his forehead.

"We have a marshal with an excellent reputation," Dr. Clagg went on, "but he is also a marshal who is willing to go along with what the townspeople accept, and within those limits, to keep the peace. That has been the customary practice in most western communities. It remains to be seen whether that is sufficient here."

The outer door opened and closed, then the door to the

inner office opened, and Laine Tennison stood there. "Rupert," she said abruptly, "I believe this meeting concerns me. I wish to join it."

"I was expecting you," Clagg said. "I told Dottie to let you know what was happening. Will you sit down?"

Tom Hayes started to get up, then sat down again. "Now look, Doc," he protested, "I ain't sure I want to get mixed up in this. Things have been going along pretty good, and—"

"Hold your horses, Tom," Billy Townsend said easily. "You just set still and listen to what the Doc has to say. He looks to me like a man with ideas."

Hayes glanced around uneasily, but sat back in his chair. "What about her?" he grumbled. "What's that girl doin' in here?"

Laine turned on him coolly. "I am here because I have a bigger stake in this than any of you. I own the mines—both of them."

All eyes turned toward her and she colored a little, her chin lifting.

"That's right, gentlemen," Clagg said. "Miss Tennison has another distinction. She is the niece of Eli Patterson, the man whose murder started all this."

Hayes started at the word "murder," then he relaxed.

"We are here to make a decision," Clagg said. "Do we wish to continue to live upon the proceeds of crime and murder, to rear our families in an atmosphere of the acceptance of crime, getting in deeper and deeper each day; or are we going to make a break with the past and demand that this town be cleaned up?"

Billy Townsend crossed one knee over the other, and said, "If we start cleaning up this town, a lot of people are going to get hurt."

Laine Tennison spoke up sharply. "Gentlemen, let me tell you this: somebody is going to get hurt anyway. My attorneys have drafted a letter to the governor—I believe he is Jack Moorman's son-in-law—asking that a special officer be appointed to bring law and order to Rafter. I have requested a complete investigation."

She paused, looking slowly around the room. "I have requested an investigation into the stealing of gold, and also as to the identity of those who have been receiving the stolen goods." There was a stir of apprehension in the room, but she added, "However, I have no wish to bring trouble to anybody else if I can convict those responsible and recover my gold."

"That's fair," Townsend said.

"Prosecutin' is one thing," Hayes said, "convictin' is another. Anyway, who is goin' to be the one to roust that outfit out of here?"

"If he is told to do it by the townspeople, and if he has support, I think Wilson Hoyt will do it."

"He'll try," Townsend agreed.

"He's only one man," Hayes said, "only one man against that bunch of fighters Ben Stowe has imported. Why, half of those miners are no more miners than you or me. They're pistol-men from Texas or wherever."

"Gentlemen," Clagg said dryly, "if we vote to act now, I shall myself walk beside Hoyt."

They looked at him in surprise, all but Townsend. "I run a saloon, and the money has been good. All the same, I've known it was the wrong way to run a town. Doc, when you walk out there with Hoyt, I'll be right alongside of you."

"Good," Clagg said. "I had an idea that's where you'd be, Billy."

"And me too," Fields said. "I haven't shot a rifle since the War Between the States, but I've got a mighty good shotgun."

Tom Hayes got up quickly. "You're a pack of fools!" he exclaimed angrily. "I'll have nothing to do with this."

At the back of the room two others rose quickly and ducked out the door.

Hayes hesitated, as if wanting to say something more. "You can't ride the fence, Tom," Townsend said quietly. "We called you in to give you your chance."

"Chance! Why you ain't got no chance at all. The minute Ben Stowe hears about this you'll all be riding for a slab on Boot Hill!"

Billy Townsend was smiling a little. "Are you going to tell him, Tom?"

Hayes flushed angrily. "No, I ain't! And don't come blamin' me if he hears of it!" He went out the door and closed it quickly after him.

For a moment there was silence, and then Pete Hillaby stood up. "You can count me in, Doc. I'll stand with you."

In the end, there were nine men left. Doctor Rupert Clagg glanced from one to another. "All right, boys. From this moment we go armed, and no one of us is to be alone. You'll get the word from Billy here, and we'll all meet at his place. In the meantime I'll have a talk with Wilson Hoyt."

When all of them had left, Dr. Clagg turned to Laine. "Well, we've made a start, and I believe we'll carry it off."

"With only nine men?" Laine was frightened. "Rupert, we've got to get word to Mike Shevlin before anything happens."

"He's a tough man—we could use him," Clagg agreed. He hesitated. "I'll ride out and get him."

"No," Laine protested. "You stay here. If you ride out there everyone will know something is happening. I'll go get him."

And at last he agreed, for there was much to do in Rafter, and very little time.

Laine Tennison rode her dapple-gray mare out of town toward Parry's claim, following only a few minutes behind Ben Stowe. She rode swiftly, keeping in mind the location of Parry's claim, for the mining maps of the area that she had studied for hours were clearly fixed in her memory. The trail to the claim was round about, although the actual distance, as the crow flies, was quite short.

Finally she turned into the narrow canyon. It was not hard to recognize the mountain in which the two mines were located, and she knew at once the mouth of the discovery tunnel when she saw it. Though the tunnel had not been used, it was clearly indicated on her maps.

As she rode up to the claim, the first thing she saw was Ben Stowe's horse. Stowe was nowhere in sight, and neither was Burt Parry or Mike Shevlin.

Laine stood very still and looked across the canyon. There was the dump at the discovery claim. And then she suddenly knew where they were.

She went to her saddlebag and got her pistol.

FIFTEEN

When he was well within the tunnel, Mike Shevlin paused to light his candle, then placed it in the holder on his cap. Although he had worked underground, he had never cared much for it; and he hesitated now, knowing the traps that might lie before him.

As he went forward, he counted his steps, and when he had gone fifty paces into the tunnel he paused to listen, but there was no sound. He tilted his head back, letting the light play on the rock overhead. It looked solid. The chances were that if this place was in use at all, somebody was barring down to prevent loose rock from falling.

He walked on a little further, and an ever so slight bend in the drift cut him off from the spot of light that was the mouth of the tunnel. Suddenly he saw the ladder of a manway, and beyond it the end of the drift. The ladder led upward into the darkness.

Again he listened.

There was no sound but the slow drip of water near the end of the drift. He turned and started up the ladder.

Then he thought he heard the sound of a single-jack, somewhere far off, but the sound ceased almost at once and he was not sure about it. He paused again, looking up the ladder, remembering how Laine's investigator had been caught in just such a place by falling drills. The long steel shafts must have gone clear through him . . . it was an unpleasant thought.

Suddenly he saw the opening of a drift on his left. The ladder continued on upward, but he stepped off and stood on the platform at the lip of the manway. He listened, but could hear nothing; then, squatting on his heels, he studied the planks of the platform. The dust was thick, and undisturbed.

Obviously this area was unworked, yet the flame of his candle indicated a slight movement of air. Somewhere down that tunnel there was an opening, either from the drift he was in, or from a connecting one.

He felt nervous and jumpy. This was different from facing a man with a gun in the open air. Here it was dark and still, a place where a man without a light would be helpless. For anyone who had never worked underground it was always a shock to realize the complete absence of light, the utter blackness, deep in a mine or a cave. There is no such thing as the eyes growing accustomed to absolute darkness . . . there one is completely blind.

Anyone he might meet down here would have the advantage of knowing the mine—he would know every manway, every cross-cut, raise, or winze. He would know where to go and how to get there. Mike, a stranger to the mine, might find himself in an old stope or a waste-fill from which there was no escape.

He turned back to the ladder and began climbing, but he paused after only a few steps. He was perspiring profusely, and he knew it was not from heat—it was from fear.

Mike Shevlin had known fear before: only a man who was a fool could say that he had never been afraid. On that manway Shevlin would be almost helpless if someone decided to do to him what they had done to the other investigator. And nobody could prove it was anything but an accident.

He had climbed only fifty feet when he heard voices, and far above him he saw a faint glimmer of light. Someone was coming toward him.

To go back down was impossible in the time he had, but right above him, on his left, another drift opening showed, black and empty. With quick steps he was up the ladder and into the dark opening. He had an instant, no more, in which to see that he stood on a "station" about twenty feet across; opposite him the drift disappeared into the depths of the mountain.

There was no time to hesitate, for already he could hear feet on the ladder. He took off his cap and pinched out the light. And then, in absolute blackness, he tiptoed across to the tunnel. He missed the opening by a few feet, but he found it and had only just got inside when he saw the glimmer of light nearing the station he had just abandoned.

Feeling his way along the wall of the drift, he worked his way deeper into the mine, hoping for a cross-cut that would enable him to get out of sight. The men on the ladder might go on down, but if they stopped he was in trouble.

They stopped.

Flattened against the wall of the drift, he waited. He could hear the murmur of voices, and in another moment a man came into sight—a stocky, powerful-looking man lighting a pipe. The second man followed. Neither man seemed to be armed with anything but a pick-handle, though that was quite enough in case of a hand-to-hand fight in the mine.

At first Shevlin could hear only snatches of their conversation. Obviously, they had stopped off on the station to have a smoke . . . but what would they do when they finished that? Would they come along the drift toward him?

". . . jumpy. I tell you, Al, I don't like the looks of it. You been down to the Nevada House since? Or the Blue Horn?"

Shevlin could not distinguish the words of the other man, but the first one spoke again. "Well, I was down there, and there wasn't nobody around. That's a bad sign. I tell you, I can smell vigilantes. I seen this happen before. You can raise all the hell you want, rob a man, or even kill one, and nobody says much; but you bother a woman or do one any harm, and folks change."

There was another indistinguishable comment, and then: "You may not be worried, but I am. And I ain't the only one. The boss is worried, too. You watched him lately? He's jumpy as a cat."

Presently they returned to the manway and went on down. Shevlin waited for them to be well away, then he struck a match and lighted his cap-lamp.

He walked on along the drift, passing several cross-cuts, and once a bank of four ore chutes, thick with dust and long unused.

His uneasiness increased with every step. He knew he was walking into trouble, and the last thing he wanted was trouble underground. In such a place it was always risky to use a gun, for the concussion might bring down some rock, especially in a long-worked area.

It seemed obvious that the two men were guards following a regular patrol, and they might appear again at any time.

He had never seen a working plan of the mine, and had no idea how extensive the workings were. There was now a continual drip of water, and here and there were shallow pools.

Suddenly he came to a cross-cut. A few feet in, on one side, was a heavy plank door, which he found was locked.

This could be a powder room, but he had never seen one built with such care. The heavy planks had been set back into the rock on either side and strengthened by huge twelve-by-twelve posts. He took hold of the handle of the door, but it was so solid that it could neither be moved nor shaken. And it was fitted so snugly that it offered no place for a bar or wedge. His guess was that the planks were three-by-twelves—and short of a battering ram or dynamite, such a door could not be forced. Half an hour's work with a good axe might do the job—but even so, there might be a guard posted somewhere on the other side of the door.

This then, had to be the opening into the area from which they were mining the high-grade ore.

The cross-cut beyond the drift on the other side was half filled with waste. The main drift led on into the mountain, and he surmised he was almost halfway through to the side toward Rafter Crossing.

Thoughtfully, Shevlin studied the rock in which the door was framed, but it appeared to be as solid as the mountain of which it was a part. He stood there a moment, reluctant to give up, and attempted to visualize his present position in terms of the two mine shafts. But a man's movement underground can be deceptive, and he could not be sure.

As he hesitated, he felt a growing sense of uneasiness, a disturbing feeling that he was watched. Was there a peekhole, somehow disguised, in the door itself? He shrugged and turned away, his cap-lamp throwing a feeble glow around him.

He walked back to the main drift and stopped there, wondering if he dared go deeper into the mine. At the same time, from the corner of his eye, he glimpsed something that sent a chill through him.

On top of the piled-up waste rock in the other side of the cross-cut was a rifle muzzle, and he had no doubt at all that somebody lay behind it, ready to shoot if necessary.

An interesting gleam from the wall of the drift caught his eye, and he stepped over to it, making a pretense of studying the rock. He knocked off a corner with the prospector's pick he carried in his belt and examined it in the light from his cap-lamp. As he studied it, he tried to think what it was best to do.

The obvious thing to do was to turn and walk back down the drift the way he had come. If he did so, his presence might be passed off as a harmless exploring of an old mine-working. Under the circumstances it was highly improbable, but it just might work. On the other hand, would the hidden watcher allow him to go? Might he not shoot at any moment?

Shevlin started to turn away when he heard, from down the drift, along the way he himself had come, the sound of boots. Someone was coming toward him, someone who could be no great distance away. Quickly, Shevlin turned and went up the drift toward the main working of the mine, and he had gone no more than fifty feet before he came to another row of four ore chutes and a manway.

There was only time to observe that the dust on the ladder was undisturbed, and then he was climbing, swiftly and silently. Not thirty feet above, he entered a stope where the ore had been mined out and shot down from overhead. Crawling over the heaped-up rock, he crouched down in a small hollow and waited, listening.

The place where he had chosen to hide was right at the top of an empty chute where his slightest movement might be heard below, but where he himself could hear what went on down there. He heard the distant footsteps, then came a pause. Watching over the rim of the chute, his own light placed on the muck well behind him, he saw the faint movement of the walker's light, but he heard no voices.

What of the man behind the gun? Was he equally unknown to whoever had come along the tunnel?

Suddenly, he heard a faint gasp, and then the rustle of clothing. Someone whose feet and legs he could see, scurried past the chute and stepped into the space between that chute and the next. Shevlin could hear again the rustle of denim against the framework of the chute. And then, very faintly, he heard still other steps.

This was impossible, and yet it was happening. Three men were now in hiding in the old mine-working all within a few yards of the great plank door!

The new steps came on, hesitated, then continued on again. They, too, paused when they faced that solidly framed door. Breathing ever so faintly, Shevlin watched over the edge of the chute, watched the reflection of distant light; in a moment whoever it was who held the light came on up the drift that ran past the chutes.

Suddenly, the man below stirred, and stepped quickly out into the tunnel.

"Well, now. Fancy seein' you here!" That was Ben Stowe's voice. "A mine is no place for a lady. Would you mind tellin' me what you're lookin' for?"

"Oh! You frightened me. Aren't you Ben Stowe?" It was Laine Tennison who spoke. "I've never been in a mine before— there's so much I'd like to know, and I don't believe Dr. Clagg would have the time to show me around. Would you tell me about the mine, Mr. Stowe? For instance, what are these things?"

She craned her neck and looked up the chute, and there was an instant when Mike Shevlin was sure she had seen him, just an instant before he pulled his head back.

"That's an ore chute," Stowe answered. "The rock is shot down off the walls and roof up there in the stope, and then pulled out of that chute into a car and trammed—pushed—outside."

His boots shifted on the rock below. "Ma'am," he went on, "what are you doing in this mine? What's your business here?"

"Business? Oh, I've no business here, Mr. Stowe. I just saw the tunnel and thought I'd look in. Do they mine gold here? Or is it silver? I don't know very much about mining, I'm afraid, but it all looks very exciting."

"How do you happen to be out here, anyway?"

"Here? Oh, you mean in the canyon? I was looking for Mr. Shevlin. Dr. Clagg wanted to see him; and Mrs. Clagg and I . . . well, we thought we would invite him for supper. He's very good-looking—don't you think so, Mr. Stowe?"

"I never noticed." Ben Stowe was obviously puzzled, and Shevlin could scarcely restrain a chuckle. She was trying, trying hard, but would it work? Would she appear so much the rattle-brained female that Stowe would let her go?

"You're very handsome yourself, Mr. Stowe. Would you like to come to supper? It's nothing fancy. I mean, well, after all it's just *supper*, not a dinner or anything fancy. So you'd have to take potluck, but I do so admire western men, and I don't know if I'll find Mr. Shevlin, but even if I do, you're welcome. In fact, we'd simply adore having you."

Stowe started to speak, but she gave him no chance. "Why, just the other day Dottie was saying—Dottie, that's Mrs. Clagg— that she couldn't understand why some girl hadn't set her cap for you. You're so *successful* and all."

"Ma'am, where'd you get that candle?" was Ben Stowe's response. "Looks to me like you came fixed for looking at mines."

"Oh, *this?* I found it in that cabin there, Burt Parry's cabin. I didn't think he'd mind if I—you don't think he'd mind do you, Mr. Stowe? I mean, I just *borrowed* it. I'll put it right back where I found it." She paused only a moment.

"Mr. Stowe . . . or may I call you Ben? Would you take me back to town? I mean, it must be getting dark outside, and if you would take me home I'd be ever so glad . . . I mean, it wouldn't be too much trouble, would it?"

"No, no trouble," Stowe answered.

Mike Shevlin, crouching, his legs cramped and aching, heard

their footsteps retreating down the drift. He waited for what he felt was a safe time, and then, with great care to make no sound, he straightened up, took up his cap, and walked to the manway. All was dark and still down below. Softly, he went down the ladder and tiptoed along the drift.

Far down the tunnel he could see two bobbing lights. After waiting until they disappeared, he crept forward. With gun in hand, he deliberately looked toward the cross-cut where he had seen the rifle muzzle. It was gone.

Scrambling up the pile of muck, he peered over behind it. There was a snug nest among the rocky debris that had been pitched into the tunnel, and scattered here and there among the rocks were crumbs and bits of food. Someone had been waiting here for quite some time; perhaps, by the look of the place, for days or even weeks.

Where had this person gone? Had he slipped away down the drift while Ben Stowe talked to Laine? It seemed to be the only explanation, for if the heavy door had been opened it would surely have made some sound, or some change in the draught of air moving through the mine.

At the opening of the tunnel, his light snubbed out, Mike Shevlin paused and waited, listening, but he heard no sound.

He stepped outside, and not until he was beside his horse did he allow himself to take a long, deep breath of the clean, fresh air. It was good to be alive . . . very good indeed.

And then he thought of Laine Tennison. Ben Stowe was a sharp customer . . . how long would he be fooled? Or was he fooled at all?

Perhaps even now . . .

SIXTEEN

Mike Shevlin checked his Winchester and shoved it down in the boot. Then he started his horse down the canyon. He was thinking that the man behind that muck pile in the cross-cut must have been Burt Parry. Not a word had passed between him and Ben Stowe . . . did Stowe know he was there?

And then Shevlin went on to think of his real problem. How could he get the gold from behind that door? First, he would have to get rid of Burt Parry, somehow; and if Parry had been chosen to guard that gold he must be a more salty customer than he appeared to be.

With Parry out of the way, the door would have to be blasted open, or cut open with an axe . . . and then what? A half-million in gold, if that was what there was in there, is not a matter to be handled with ease. Gold is heavy, and a half-million isn't something you put in your pocket.

Darkness was upon him now; the stars came out, and a low wind blew from off the sagebrush levels where the cattle grazed. Somewhere ahead of him were Laine Tennison and Ben Stowe.

Eve Bancroft, Gib Gentry, and Lon Court were dead, all killed since he had arrived in town, and yet the problem of the gold was no nearer a solution. Ben Stowe still sat snugly in his office, surrounded by his miners, who were gunfighters.

And back of all this was the major mystery: Who had killed Eli Patterson?

Lights were shining in the windows when Shevlin rode into town. He stabled his horse, and started over to the Bon Ton. He was dead-tired, and hungry. No matter what, he was going to eat now, and then he was going to his room in the Nevada House and get some sleep.

He got to the boardwalk and started toward the door of the

restaurant, when it opened suddenly and Burt Parry stepped out. When he saw Shevlin his face seemed to stiffen.

"You! Shevlin!" His voice was brusque, and even as he spoke he was putting his hand in his vest pocket.

He held out several coins to Shevlin. "Your wages. I'm going to quit the claim."

Before Mike could speak he turned his back on him and strode away, walking swiftly.

Puzzled, Shevlin opened the restaurant door and stepped inside. Tom Hayes was there, a man whom he knew by sight, and at a table in the far corner sat Clagg Merriam.

Merriam glanced up, but looked away quickly.

Mike Shevlin ordered his meal, and gratefully drank his coffee. It was hot, black, and strong. Suddenly the door opened and Ben Stowe came in. He shot a glance at Merriam, then went over to where Tom Hayes sat.

"I didn't know you and Doc Clagg were such friends, Tom," Stowe said quietly. "Heard you were seeing him today. Or are you sick?"

"Poorly." Hayes' face was haggard. "I been feelin' poorly."

"Too bad. I figured it was something like that. Well, what else can you expect? A doctor is usually dealing with people who live unhealthy lives." Stowe slapped Hayes heavily on the back. "Don't worry about it, Ben. What's a little stomachache when so many people are dying?"

Ben Stowe's eyes shifted to Mike Shevlin, and he crossed over to his table. "Mind if I sit down, Mike?" he said genially.

Hayes got up and left the restaurant hurriedly, and Stowe looked after him, contempt in his eyes.

When he was seated, Stowe took out two cigars, held out one to Shevlin and lighted the other for himself.

"Mike," he said, "I've been giving it some thought. We were pretty close in the old days, you and me, and with Gib gone I'm going to need a man." His voice lowered. "I'm going to need a man who has guts and a gun. But one who won't stampede."

"You're talking," Shevlin said. He was so tired that he felt he could hardly keep his eyes open.

"I figure a man can always use some money, and you were one who could take it when the chance offered. What would you say to stepping into Gib's shoes at the express company?"

Their voices were so low that it would not have been possible for anyone else to hear them. The offer seemed to be dropped casually by Stowe, but he added, almost as an afterthought, "There would be a tidy bit coming after this is all over. Gib worked for it, but now he won't be with us, so why shouldn't you pick up where he left off?"

"I wouldn't want to end up like Gentry did, Ben."

Stowe brushed off the suggestion with a wave of the cigar-holding hand. "You can take care of yourself. Anyway, I need you. I needed Gib, for that matter. His getting shot was all a mistake."

Shevlin looked up at Stowe. "You're damn' right it was, and I know just what kind of mistake."

Ben Stowe chuckled. "Figured you did. But look, Mike, we're playing for big money here. You can't blame a man for covering all the angles. Now with Gib gone, things are different. I need you. Gib's end could have come to that freight line, plus half a million dollars . . . *half a million dollars, Mike!* How long is it going to take you to make that much money?"

Mike Shevlin was thoroughly awake now. "Just what has to be done to make that kind of money?" he asked.

Stowe held his cigar in his hand. "Mike, I'm going to level with you. After all, you've been up the creek and over the mountain, and you can read sign as well as the next man. I need somebody to handle some freight shipments, somebody tough enough to take those shipments through—regardless of what happens."

"You think I can do it?"

"Like nobody else. Better than Gib, even."

"Do you think somebody will try to stop a shipment?"

Stowe leaned his big forearms on the table. "You're damn' tootin', I do. Where do you think Ray Hollister is right now?"

Weariness was creeping over him, but he forced his mind to consider Stowe's offer, an offer so astonishing he could scarcely believe it. The gold was to be placed right in his hands. He wouldn't have to look for it; he would have it in his charge—but under the suspicious guns of Ben's gunmen.

Half a million dollars . . . that would be better than ten per cent of half a million. Undoubtedly some would be in cash; the rest of the half-million to come from later mining.

He would be a rich man, free to do as he chose, and no strings attached. Of course, Ben Stowe planned to have him killed, but two could play at this game. Suppose he killed Ben Stowe? He would have all the gold for himself.

He looked at Stowe. "Ben, it sounds like a good deal. You let me sleep on it."

He got up from the table and went towards the door, where he paused a moment. "After all, where else would I get a chance at that much money?"

After he had gone, Stowe stared at the door, an ugly look in his eyes. "He's lying," he said; "that two-by-four gunfighter is lying. He thinks he can outfigure me. Well, I'll show him . . . but first, he'll take that gold out for me."

He spoke aloud, but not loudly enough to be heard by either Clagg Merriam or the waitress. He sat there alone for several minutes, studying the case in all its aspects. He could find no alternative. Hollister was out there somewhere, and he was the kind who would have to be killed, sooner or later. Hollister never knew when he was whipped, or when he had no chance of winning. Moreover, Hollister, fool that he was in personal relations, was shrewd enough when it came to figuring the angles; and Babcock was with him.

If there was a man in the Rafter country who could outguess Hollister, it was Mike Shevlin. And then he would, personally, kill Shevlin.

The thought gave Stowe a sudden deep satisfaction. He realized that he hated Shevlin, and, come to think of it, he always had. Mike Shevlin was the only one who had never accepted his leadership. Gib Gentry had been ready enough, but not Shevlin.

A shadow loomed beside his table. He tilted his head back and looked up into the hard but handsome face of Merriam.

"Hello, Clagg. Sit down."

Merriam remained standing. "You're taking a long chance, Ben." Merriam's voice was even. "Shevlin's got only one thing on his mind. He wants the man who killed Patterson."

Ben Stowe shrugged, his face unreadable. "So? We need Shevlin—we use him, then we take care of him."

"Who does?"

Ben smiled. "Why, I do. I reserve the privilege for myself. That's one thing you can have no part of, Merriam."

"I had a letter today . . . from the governor," Merriam said.

"I didn't know you two were friends?"

"We're not, not exactly. I supported him for the office. Made a contribution."

"Then why worry? Tell him everything is all right in Rafter."

"He knows better—and believe me, that contribution doesn't mean a thing. That indicated support of his policies, but it didn't buy immunity from a crime."

Ben Stowe knew he had to be careful. Merriam had been touchy of late. Was he running scared? Was this thing getting under his skin? The worst of it was, he needed Merriam, needed him for a little while, anyway.

"Sit down," he said again, "and keep your voice down." He

leaned his arms on the table. "Look, I'm going to make a deal for Shevlin to take the stuff out, and when he gets it where it goes . . . payoff."

"Will he listen to you?"

Stowe's face showed a grim smile. "Up to a point, any man will listen to money. What he's asking himself right now is how he can get away with all of it. And don't you be worried about Eli Patterson. He's a long time dead, and half a million in gold is a lot of money. Mike Shevlin never had anything in his whole life but a horse and a gun, and here's his big chance. He'll go along."

"I don't like killing."

"So you've said before, but Shevlin will die a long way from here."

At this moment, at the hotel, Mike Shevlin was stripping off his clothes, and he almost fell into bed. He was nearly asleep already when he pulled the blankets over him.

But Laine Tennison lay wide awake in her bed at Dr. Clagg's house, staring up into the darkness. She was remembering the face she had seen at the top of the chute in the mine, just barely seen. She had talked fast to get Ben Stowe out of there, talked glibly to get him to bring her home, but she was worried about him. How much had he been fooled by her chatter? She was afraid he had not been fooled at all.

Of one thing she was sure: Ben Stowe was the most ruthless man she had ever met. She had not the slightest doubt that he had ordered Lon Court to kill her, or that he would kill her when the opportunity offered, and if he was sure of the need for it.

The death of Eve Bancroft had dampened a lot of the spirits around Rafter Crossing. One man in town who lay wide awake was Tom Hayes. Stowe's talk with Hayes had frightened him, and he lay awake now, remembering the veiled threats Stowe had delivered to him in the restaurant.

All his life Hayes had lived in the shadow of mightier men, and he envied them not at all, for to be mighty was to be a target for hatred. He had carefully avoided facing issues, avoided taking sides, avoided making decisions that might lead to trouble. And now, through the invitation of Dr. Clagg, he himself had become vulnerable. And he was frightened.

He got up suddenly and reached for his pants.

SEVENTEEN

Laine Tennison awakened with a start, every sense alert. She did not sit up, she did not even stir, only her eyes were wide and she was listening.

Her room was very dark, for there was no moon at this hour. There was no wind, but she had a feeling of movement, of stirring. Somewhere in the house a board creaked. Was Rupert having a late night call?

Immediately, she knew that would not be true, for at such times Dottie never failed to get up and start a fire for some tea. There was something wrong, definitely wrong.

Very quietly, she listened, and heard a voice, not loud but clear enough. "Doc, you take it easy now. I'd surely hate to kill the only doctor in the country around. You sit tight, and nobody will get hurt."

She knew the voice. It was that man they called Red, and he worked for Ben Stowe. Somehow Ben Stowe must have discovered the move they were about to make against him, and he was taking steps to prevent it.

Where was Brazos, she wondered. But as she asked herself the question, she remembered: Rupert Clagg had sent him out of town, carrying a message to two ranchers Clagg believed might join them to throw Stowe out. He was to go to Walt Kelly's place first, and then across country to Joe Holiday's.

Who had the others been? There were Billy Townsend and Fields, and if they had not been taken, they must be warned, and quickly. She turned swiftly and went to the window, which was partly raised. Ever so gently, she lifted the window still further.

Was someone on watch out there? It was likely. She went

over the sill very quietly, and stood still a moment. How much time did she have before they would come to her room?

There was a man standing near the gate, so she went quickly along the edge of the lilac bushes, hesitated, then moved swiftly across a small open space to the shadow of the barn. There was no chance of getting a horse, but for what she intended to do, a horse was unnecessary.

At the back of the barn was a small gate, and she opened it softly and went through, closed it, and took the same route Mike Shevlin had once used to approach the house. Hurrying, running and walking, she reached an alley that led to the street.

The town was in darkness; the only lights were at the Blue Horn, in the rooms at the back where Townsend lived. Two men were loafing on the boardwalk out front.

If Ben Stowe had discovered Rupert's plans, he must also know that Laine Tennison owned the mines. She had to have somewhere to hide, some place where she would not be found. And in her need she had thought of Mike Shevlin's room in the Nevada House.

He would not be there, but she knew he had kept the room, for he was often in town. This time, as before, she went to the back of the hotel and went up the outside stairs to the second floor.

The hall was empty. She went along it swiftly, praying his door would be unlocked. It was, and she stepped inside quickly. At the same moment she felt the sharp prod of a gun in her ribs.

"Mike?" she whispered.

"Yes," he said softly. "What's happened?"

As rapidly as she could, she explained what had taken place, from the meeting at the house until now.

"There wasn't a chance for them to carry it out, Mike. I don't believe Rupert had even talked to Mr. Hoyt. I was going to tell you about it when I rode out to the claim, but you were gone, and I couldn't resist looking into that tunnel. And then Ben Stowe was there, and when I saw you I couldn't think of anything but getting him out of there."

"Did you see anybody else? Anybody outside or inside the mine?"

"No . . . no one at all."

He scarcely realized what she said, for he was thinking of Ben Stowe, wondering what Stowe would do. Now that he knew who would be against him, would he kill them all? But then, how could the disappearance of several prominent citizens be explained? Or would he just hold them, try to put the fear of death into them, then let them go?

Shevlin's every sense told him that Ben Stowe was riding the rim right now. He had killed, and killed more than once. He had gotten away with it, and with his success had come that sense of power that comes to such men, the feeling that they can go on killing and remain immune. In such men, the ego grew and grew, until they rode rough-shod over every obstacle.

Yet Stowe had always been a coldly cautious man. There had never been anything of the reckless, heedless, hell-for-leather cowhand in him. How much had his character changed?

"Laine, you've got to hide," Shevlin said now. "You've got to stay out of sight, and this is the best place I can think of. There's some grub in my duffel—it isn't much, but your best bet is to stay right here where they won't dream of hunting you."

"And you?"

"I'm taking the gold out, Laine. Ben Stowe offered me a deal—he offered me Gentry's piece of the operation."

Her eyes searched his face. "That could mean a lot, couldn't it?"

He took her by the shoulders. "Yes," he agreed, "it could mean a lot. He'll try to kill me; in fact, he will probably try before I reach the end of the trip, or at any rate, just after I do; but if I can stay with it, I could come out of it a rich man. The only thing is, it wouldn't give me what I want most."

"And what would that be?"

"You."

She made no effort to draw away from him, no effort to escape his hands. She just looked up at him, her eyes cool and almost appraising.

He had thought of her, too often, these past few days and had called himself a fool for thinking what he did. He had told himself over and over that he would never have the nerve to say anything to her; but now here it was, and he had said it, and she was not laughing at him. That was something, at least.

"Mike," she was saying, "how are you going to manage it?"

"I'm going out with them. I'm going to take that gold out, and somehow or other I've got to stay alive and keep that gold for you. Right now everything hinges on it."

"Mike, I'm afraid."

"You just wait here. I'll be back. If Ben Stowe doesn't have that gold, he doesn't have anything. He can't buy the mine, he can't pay off his men; everything will fall apart for him and for

Clagg Merriam too. Merriam's mortgaged everything to put up the money to buy the gold."

"They will fight."

"Yes, I think so."

"Then be careful. You'll be all alone, Mike."

He looked at her and smiled, a little wistfully. "When haven't I been alone?" he said.

"Wasn't there ever anybody, anybody at all?"

"No . . . not really. Maybe that was why I kept moving. It's easier to be alone if you keep moving, because it seems natural not to know people or be close to anybody in strange country."

"Mike," she pleaded, "please don't go. Let's just ride away from here. We can go to the capital and talk to the governor, then let him investigate."

"Laine, by that time they'd have your gold out of here and everything covered up. You might get Ben Stowe out of his job and take the mines back, but you can be sure he'd dynamite the approaches to the high-grade, so that you might spend all you have just looking for it—at least he'd try."

Mike Shevlin hesitated, and then he said, "Laine, I came here to find out the truth about Eli Patterson, to clear his name, and to put the man who killed him where he should be—in prison."

"You'd not kill him?"

"Not unless he pushed it on me. The law is coming to this country, and the sooner the better. Men can't live without law, and each of us should do his part to help the men who enforce it. After all, they are our servants, and without them we'd live in anarchy. Take it from me, because I've seen it both ways."

At the door he paused. "Keep that gun close by, and don't answer the door if anybody knocks."

He went out, and the door closed behind him. He was gone from the hall before she realized she had forgotten to bring her gun with her.

She propped a chair under the doorknob, then she sat down on the bed, and took off her shoes.

She must make no noise. It would not do to have anyone wondering who was in Mike Shevlin's room after he had gone out.

It was no use to worry about Dottie Clagg, either. Dottie would be frightened, and worried sick, but if Laine went back to the doctor's house she would only bring more trouble with her. She must trust in Shevlin, and wait.

She considered Shevlin. Although almost nothing personal had passed between them, a feeling existed that needed no words. From the first, she had been drawn to him. Lean and savage as he was, there was an odd gentleness in him, too, and a curious respect for her.

She tried to recall everything Uncle Eli had said about him, and thinking of this, she lay back on the bed. She did not see the knob turn slowly, did not hear the slight creak as pressure was put on the door to open it.

The chair under the knob remained firm, and the person outside the door ceased trying. Had she been awake, she might have heard his breathing, might have heard the soft creak of the floor boards as he retreated down the hall. But she was fast asleep.

EIGHTEEN

Rafter Crossing crouched in the darkness like a waiting cat. And like a waiting cat, its eyes missed nothing—or almost nothing. Mike Shevlin, refreshed after only three hours of sleep, walked toward the lighted window of Ben Stowe's office. Around him there was a rustle of movement in the night— nothing a man could actually hear if he stopped to listen, but something of which he would be keenly aware.

Ben Stowe looked up when the door opened, and his eyes became wary when he recognized Mike Shevlin.

Mike leaned his big fists on the table. "Ben," he said, "I'll move your gold if you have it ready before daybreak."

Stowe rolled his cigar in his mouth while he took a minute to consider what this might mean. What had happened to settle Shevlin's mind so quickly? Could he have heard of the seizure of Doc Clagg and his party? That was unlikely because, as Stowe happened to know, Shevlin had gone to his hotel and had not left it until now.

"Look at it this way, Ben," Mike continued. "If Hollister is still around, he will have spies in town. I've a hunch they won't suspect me, but if we start now we can get into safe country before Hollister can get word and start moving."

"That's likely," Ben agreed. He sat back in his chair and looked up at Shevlin. "Have you got any men you want to take along?"

"No, that's your play. I'll ramrod the job, you furnish the men. Let's face it, Ben. With Gentry gone, I don't have a friend in the country. I'll take my cut from this deal and ride out."

"All right, Mike. You be at the mouth of Parry's canyon an hour from now. The gold will be there."

122

"I'll want pack mules—thirty or forty of them. That much gold, at present prices, will weigh a ton."

"Any special reason for mules rather than a wagon?"

"They'll be looking for a wagon, and I can take mules where no wagon could go." Shevlin lowered his voice. "I'm going over the ridge, Ben."

"You're crazy! There's no trail."

"Ben, I punched cows all over this country, much more than you ever did, and I know a trail that even Ray Hollister won't know."

"All right."

Ben pushed back his chair and stood up. "Don't try anything, Mike. I need you, but I don't trust you. You go along with me, and you'll be in at the payoff. But try a double-cross, and you won't live twenty-four hours."

"Don't be foolish, Ben. Where else could I get that kind of money?"

Shevlin walked to the door, then turned. "By the way, Ben, who is Burt Parry? Is he your man?"

"Parry? Just an eastern pilgrim who thinks he knows mining." Suddenly Ben Stowe read something else into the question. "Why do you ask?"

"Just wondered, that's all. That claim where he had me working . . . there isn't a sign of mineral over there, and I don't think there ever was."

When Mike Shevlin had gone, Stowe sat very still for a long time. He smoked his cigar for a while, then let it go out, and chewed for a while longer on the dead butt.

Burt Parry had seemed so much what he was supposed to be that after a few days of doubt, Stowe had largely ignored him. From time to time he heard that Parry was having a drink with Clagg Merriam, but it seemed of no importance. Clagg had lived much of his life in the East, and Parry was an easterner, so what was more natural than some casual talk between them? But suppose it was more than that? Suppose Parry had been imported by Merriam? Imported for a specific job—to watch over the gold, and perhaps to handle another task later?

Stowe realized now that his contempt for Merriam had blinded him to the depths that might lie within the man. He had been so sure that he was using Merriam, that he had not considered the other side of the coin. Suppose Clagg Merriam had been using him?

He, Ben Stowe, was operator of the mines . . . yes. But if suddenly the operation was taken out of his hands, if the governor suddenly sent a corps of investigators into the area, he alone would be sitting in a vulnerable position.

True, Clagg Merriam stood to lose all he possessed if anything went wrong, but Merriam might have some ace-in-the-hole of which Stowe was unaware. And Merriam had been smart enough to plant Burt Parry in a worthless claim where he could watch the gold cache.

Ben Stowe considered his long-range plan for removing Gentry, and then using Clagg Merriam and his share of the gold as a means to establishing himself on a respectable footing in Rafter, and in the state. Folks didn't look to see how a man came by money, he told himself; they only looked to see if he had it. But he could not feel easy now.

He got up and paced the room, muttering to himself. With a thick finger he reached up and ripped open his shirt collar—the thing seemed to be choking him. Maybe he was playing the fool, with his ideas of respectability. How long could he make it stick without blowing up? He'd be better off to take the half-million and run. Why be greedy?

His eyes narrowed with thought, and he stared at the flame of the coal-oil lamp. Well, why not do it that way?

The gold train would be going over the mountain to Tappan Junction. At the Junction a railroad car was already spotted to receive it, a car that was supposed to be loaded with hides, and was, in fact, partly loaded with them.

Mike Shevlin could take the gold across the mountain if anybody could, and arrangements had already been made on the other side. Stowe had received word that his men were waiting at the Junction. The car was routed right through to the East, where the gold could most easily be disposed of . . . or enough of it, at any rate.

Stowe had taken eastern trips before, so no one would be surprised when he took the stage out of town for the railroad, carrying only one bag.

They would all see he was taking nothing with him, and they'd never believe he was cutting out. The more he thought of it, the better he liked the idea. The gold would reach the Junction about the same time he did, and there was never anybody at the Junction but the telegraph operator, or some passing cowhand who stopped by to pick up the news.

He considered the matter with care. He would write a letter of resignation to leave behind, attributing his leave-taking to the unsettled conditions, the unfortunate slaying of Eve Bancroft, and the accompanying events. That way they would have nothing on him, nothing at all. The charges down in the mine would be set off, the drifts that led into the stopes where the high-grade had been mined could be shot down, and all they could ever accuse him of would be quitting his job.

The more he thought of it, the better he liked it. He would have half a million dollars, and nobody the wiser. There were, of course, a few details to be taken care of.

He called in the men he needed and gave the necessary orders, and after that he went through his desk; all the while he was thinking of Burt Parry. The more he considered the situation, the surer he became that Parry had been posted to watch the gold; and no doubt he was still there, or somewhere close by.

Then his thoughts shifted to Clagg Merriam. What could he do about him? Even if Parry was eliminated in one way or another, Merriam would be aware within a few days that the gold had been removed, and he would raise hell.

Yet what could he do? To start any legal action would be to reveal his own part in the swindle; and Merriam was not the type to kill. Not, at least, the type to cope with Ben Stowe. So the thing to do about Merriam was simply to do nothing. Let Merriam do whatever he wished, and then Stowe would do what was necessary.

He checked his gun, thrust another into his waistband and shouldered into his coat. It was clouding up again, and looked like rain . . . so much the better. Fewer people would be riding out on a rainy night, fewer people who might see a train of mules starting over the mountain toward the Junction.

The street was empty when he went out. He stood for a moment, collar turned up against the wind, and then he crossed the street toward the livery stable. Once, on the far side of the street, he turned and looked back toward the lights of the mine. He grinned wryly. "To hell with it!" he said aloud.

Suddenly he felt free; he felt relieved, as if he had dropped a great burden.

There had been no movement in the shadows up the street, and he had seen no one. But he himself had been seen.

Jess Winkler was too canny an old hunter to reveal himself, and he held still in the shadows, his cold eyes watching Ben Stowe. And suddenly, as surely as if he had been told, Winkler knew: Ben Stowe was cashing in. He was checking out of the game, out of the town, and out of the country.

After a few minutes Winkler went to his own horse and followed Stowe at a discreet distance. At the mouth of Parry's canyon, Stowe turned in.

"By the Lord Harry," Winkler muttered, "Ray was right! He's goin' to move that gold."

Behind a low sandhill, under cover of greasewood that topped it, Winkler hunkered down to wait and watch. Scarcely an hour had gone by when the first of the mules appeared. Winkler counted forty, some of them probably carrying the grub and outfit for the guards.

He watched them trail off across the country, keeping just off the main trail. He counted nine men in the party, and Ben Stowe was not one of them. But Mike Shevlin was.

"I'd rather it had been Ben," Winkler said to himself.

He watched them for several more minutes, then went to his horse and rode wide around and headed for Hollister's camp.

In the first gray light of day, when only an arrow of red had found the clouds above, Mike Shevlin drew up and waved the first man by, with the mules following. He waved them into an opening among the enormous tumbled boulders that were piled all around. The rider hesitated, and started to speak.

"Go ahead," Shevlin said shortly. "You can't miss it."

Shevlin tugged his sombrero a little lower on his head and swore softly. The dust had settled around his shirt collar and his neck itched from dust and sweat. He was playing it by ear . . . he had no real plan—just a vague, half-formed idea that seemed to be taking shape in the back of his mind.

He knew none of these men, although two were the men he had seen inside the mine; but he knew the breed. It was a breed of tough men, men hired for their guns, or for their willingness to use violence, men working here today, and five hundred miles from here next week or the week after. Their bodies lie in many an arroyo, in unmarked boot-hill graves, or churned into mud on the grasslands of Kansas or the Indian Territory.

Some of them were good men, good in the sense of courage and physical ability, but for the most part they were men who sought what they thought of as easy money, although it rarely was. They earned three times as much as the average cowhand, and as a rule they lived a third as long.

He knew their kind, for in a sense he was one of them. The difference was that he had chosen to ride on the side of the law—and when you came down to it, that was quite a difference.

He had deeply ingrained within him a respect for the law, and the need for it. He knew that otherwise life would be a jungle, and he knew, too, that many of those who made out to

NINETEEN

When Mike Shevlin rode out of the dark pines he faced a vast green slope, perhaps a thousand acres of untouched grass, slanting away from the rounded crest of the mountain toward the dark canyon off to his left.

To his right and well ahead of him, three dark jagged crags tore at the sky, trailing drifts of wind-blown cloud like streamers of smoke. The rain was a gray veil, the grass a brilliant green, while the sky was masked with lowering thunderheads.

There was no wind on this slope shielded by the mountain, but he was chilly under the slicker; and his wet hands worried him, for if he needed a gun he would need it fast—and with accurate aim.

It took a long time to cross the wide green slope. At the end it fell sharply away into the last canyon before Stone Cabin, and he drew rein here and sat his horse, looking across at the squat gray shape, tantalized as always by the wonder of it. Who had found this wild and lonely place so long ago?

At this point he was over a mile higher than Rafter Crossing, and a good thousand feet above the trail followed by the pack mules. There might be accidents due to the weather, but there was no danger of them going astray.

Nobody he knew at Rafter had ever seen Stone Cabin, and he himself had not talked of it, wishing jealously to keep this place for himself. Many knew about the Cabin, some scarcely believing in it; but there it was, on the slope across the canyon, under the shadow of ancient trees. A dwarfish army of cedars was massed not far above it, as if waiting to leap upon it in some moment of stillness.

At last Shevlin was angling steeply down, searching out the

131

old trail, glad that he had a good mountain horse, when he saw them. At first he could not believe his eyes.

He drew up sharply, peering down at the five riders coming out of the draw, about a mile away. He saw them begin to fan out among the rocks and trees.

They were not more than a hundred yards from the trail, which at that point came out into the open for a good half-mile, just beyond the low glacial ridge where the five were taking shelter.

Their backs were to him—but for how long? If they happened to turn he could be plainly seen up here. He had to get off this slope and into the trees.

Jess Winkler . . . Of course. He should have thought of the old wolfer who had been riding these hills for years. Winkler must be down there. Nobody else could have known of the trail the mules were using; and the trail these five had taken to get here from below must be one even Shevlin knew nothing of.

He walked his horse along the slope and got into the trees without being seen. Then, screened by the dripping trees, he rode at a dead run, racing against time. If the pack train had had no trouble they would soon be along, riding like sitting pigeons into the range of Hollister's guns.

Against the five men down there, he had the nine with the pack train. But they would be scattered out along the line of mules, and the first volley would surely eliminate some of them unless they could be warned.

Hollister was a fair hand with a rifle, good with a six-gun. And Winkler—well, Winkler would never miss. When he aimed from a rest, he killed. Babcock was good too, and the others were probably at least average.

He raced his horse for about a quarter of a mile, slowed to a walk over more difficult ground, and then raced on. He came out of the trees behind Hollister and his men, and a good two hundred yards away. He could see them settled down and waiting, and just as he had spotted the fifth man, the first of the pack mules came into sight.

The first man in the pack train was a tall, lean, stoop-shouldered Texan; there were six mules before the second man appeared. In a matter of minutes they would all be strung out along the trail, and helpless. And he knew that Hollister would hold his fire until all were within easy range.

Mike Shevlin felt a curious emptiness inside him. He knew what was coming. *You could die down there,* he told himself.

He tugged on his hat brim and started down the slope behind the waiting men.

His horse walked quickly, daintily. Shevlin touched a flank lightly with a spur, and the horse began to canter. The five men below were fixing all their attention on the approaching mule train.

Suddenly one of the men with the mule train saw Shevlin, and drew up sharply. At the same instant, Shevlin shucked a six-shooter and slapped the spurs to his horse.

The startled animal almost leaped from under him, then went pounding down the slope, running like the wind. There came a startled exclamation, and one of Hollister's men whirled toward him, and Mike let go his first shot.

He was not over fifty yards off, but the shot was a clear miss, serving only to make the man jerk back, off balance, out of position for a shot.

Guns started to bark, and Shevlin saw the lean Texan in the van spur his horse up the slope. He caught on fast, that one. Mike saw one of the men lift a rifle, and then he was among them. He chopped down and shot full into the man's face, seeing it flame with blood as the bullet struck a glancing blow that knocked the man sprawling under his horse's hoofs.

Shevlin reined around quickly, glad he was riding a good cutting horse used to making quick turns. The Texan was among them too, his horse down and screaming, the man himself firing—falling and firing. Two more men came up the slope and one of them launched himself in a long dive at Winkler, and the two went rolling.

As his horse came around, Shevlin saw two more men from the pack train spurring up the slope, and then his horse, tired from the long ride, put a foot down wrong and they both fell. He rolled over, but came up still gripping a gun as Hollister ran up to face him.

"*Damn you!*" Hollister screamed. "I should have killed—"

Mike Shevlin felt the gun bucking in his hard grip, and he saw Hollister jerk as if lashed by a whip, jerk again, and fall forward on the wet slope of grass.

Hollister rolled over and started to get up, but Mike put a bullet into his chest at a range of six feet. Then he turned swiftly to face whoever was left.

The sound of the gunfire was rolling against the hills, then rolling back in echoing, muted thunder. It fell away and was lost, and there was no other sound but the rain falling, and somewhere a man groaning.

Mike picked up Hollister's unused gun, thrust it behind his belt, and walked across the grass.

John Sande was lying face down on the grass, dead. A man sitting against a rock just beyond Sande turned and looked at Shevlin. "You played hell, Mike," he said, almost without expression.

It was Babcock. His right arm was a bloody mess. Numb with shock, he was gripping his arm tightly against the flow of blood, and gazing hollow-eyed at Shevlin.

Halloran was lying dead, too, shot clean through. The Texan was dead, and two others from the mule train. There was no sign of Jess Winkler.

Down on the flat the mules were bunched, and four men, rifles ready, clustered about them. They had played it the smart way, bunching the animals and holding them tight, ready for anything.

Mike Shevlin looked carefully around. One of his men was missing, . . . probably the man who had tangled with the old wolf-hunter.

He shouted at the men with the mules, and two of them came up the slope, riding warily. "You," he said to the nearest one, "take care of that man's wounds. He's too good to die this way. You"—he indicated the other man—"catch up the horses."

He walked over to his own horse. It had gotten up, and came toward him as he approached. He mounted and rode slowly in the direction where he had seen Winkler and the other man fighting.

He saw Jess Winkler first. The old man was on his face on top of the other man, and something was gleaming from his back. Mike drew up and looked down. What he saw was the needle-sharp point of a knife, an Arkansas toothpick.

"Hey!" came a voice that was muffled. "Pull him off me! He smells worse'n a hide-skinner."

Mike swung down and, catching the wolfer by the buckskin jacket, lifted him up. The other man crawled up from where he had been sprawled between two fallen trees, wedged in by the dead wolfer's body. He was scarcely more than a boy.

"He come at me when I got up after jumpin' him, an' I wasn't set for it. I went over backwards, just a-holdin' that knife."

"You held it in the right place," Mike said. He looked with no regret at the fierce old man, cold and dangerous as any of the wolves he had hunted so long. "Are you hurt?"

"Scratched."

"Better go through their pockets and see if there's any addresses. They'll maybe have kinfolk who'd wish to know."

"They'd of had us," the boy said, "if it hadn't been for you coming a-hellin' down that slope." He thrust out his hand. "They call me Billy the Kid."

Shevlin grinned at him. "That makes four of them I've met—and you aren't Bonney."

"I ain't Claiborne, either. My name is Daniels."

Mike Shevlin walked his horse back to where Ray Hollister lay, and he sat looking down at him. "I'll tell them where you are, Ray," he said, "and if there are any who see fit to bury you, they can ride up and do it. We haven't the time."

As he looked at him, he was remembering him all down the years. When he had first known Ray Hollister he had a good working ranch, but he was never satisfied . . . he had gotten a good woman killed, and a few men, and now he lay there, come to it at last.

"String 'em out!" he yelled at the men with the mules. "We've got ten miles to go!"

Babcock had been disarmed, and his arm was bound up and in a sling. "You goin' to bury them?" he said to Mike.

"Who's got a shovel?" Mike asked. Then he added, "Bab, if you want to stay here and bury them, you can."

Babcock stared at him. "I never figured you for a unfeeling man," he said.

"I lost a lot of feeling the night Eve Bancroft died. I didn't like her, but that girl would have ridden a-blazin' into hell for Ray Hollister, and he let her go alone."

The mules were strung out and Billy Daniels was up ahead, riding point.

"What you goin' to do with me?" Babcock asked.

"Hell, I've got no place for you, and nothing against you except damn' poor judgment in bosses. Ride along with us, and when we hit the flat you cut out for Rafter."

"*Rafter?*" Babcock was incredulous. "With this arm? I'd go through hell a-gettin' there!"

"What do you think's waiting for us down there at Tappan Junction, Bab?" Shevlin said quietly. "I figure you've had yours."

They rode on a few steps, and then Mike Shevlin said, "Ben Stowe's waiting down there. He's waiting for us."

TWENTY

Two miles short of Tappan Junction the narrow trail played out, and they could see ahead of them the two buildings of the settlement in the bottom of a great basin. The twin lines of steel came out of the west and vanished into the east.

At Tappan there was a corral with a chute for loading pens, a water tank for the trains, a combination saloon, post office, and general store, and across the tracks, the telegraph office. Adjoining the office was a waiting room with two windows, furnished with a single bench and a pot-bellied stove.

No horses were in sight, but there wouldn't be—they would be in the pens. Several cattle cars and one boxcar were standing on a siding.

Mike Shevlin, weary from his long ride, stared across the flat through the drizzling rain. It lacked an hour of sundown, and darkness would come early, with that cloud-covered sky.

Beside him, drawn and pale, rode Babcock. He had lost blood, he sagged with weariness; he was not going to make it through to Rafter Crossing. He knew it now, and so did Mike Shevlin. Only an iron will and a rawhide body had brought him this far. He needed rest and care, and they were down there waiting for him, just beyond a full-scale gun battle.

"This makes it my fight, Mike," he said. "I'll ride in with you."

"Bab, what do you suppose Ben Stowe would do if you rode in there now . . . alone?"

Babcock tried to think it through. His brain was fuzzy, and it required an effort to assemble his thoughts. "Damned if I know. He'd probably ask me what happened, then he'd either shoot me or leave me be."

"You ride in there, Bab. Tell him anything he wants to

know. I'm betting he'll want to know everything you can tell him, and I don't believe he'll shoot you. Ben Stowe only kills when he thinks there's a good reason—you're out of this now, and he'll see it plain enough. Tag Murray is down there, and he's pretty good with a wound, better than some doctors I know. You ride on in."

Babcock hesitated, and glanced back at the mule train. "What about them, Mike? They're Ben's hired gunmen."

Shevlin looked at him wryly, then dug into his pocket for a cigar. It was a fresh one, and he enjoyed lighting it. "Bab," he said, "unless I miss my guess, one or more of those boys are supposed to salt me down while we're crossing the flat out there. Unless Ben is saving me for himself.

"I said Ben Stowe only killed when there was good reason, but I'll make two exceptions to that—Ray Hollister and me. He'd take pleasure in killing either of us."

"You and him were mighty thick, one time."

"Stowe and Gentry were thick; and Gentry and me, we rode saddle partners a while. But Stowe never liked me, and I never liked him."

"Mike . . . *look there!*" It was Billy Daniels who had come up to them. "That there rider on this side, *that's a woman!*"

Al, one of the men who had carried a pick-handle that day in the mine, had also come up. "That's Red on the paint—where would he get a woman?"

"Hell!" Billy spat. "That's that Tennison girl. Nobody else rides sidesaddle with the style she's got!"

Babcock glanced at Shevlin. "So there you are," he said. "Now are you goin' to ride in there, hell a-whoopin'?"

"Go on in, Bab," Mike said again. "Tell him anything he wants to know, and don't you worry none about me."

Babcock still hesitated. "Mike, I ain't up to much, but damn it, man, you're cattle! I'll ride in there with you, or I'll cover your back, whatever you're of a mind to."

Shevlin put a hand on Babcock's shoulders. "Go on in, Bab," he repeated.

Babcock touched a heel to his horse and went off across the grass.

"What's the matter with him?" Billy Daniels asked. "What was he figurin' to do?"

Mike Shevlin stepped his horse around, and they were all there, facing him, with the gold train just beyond. His eyes went from one to another, curiously, somewhat mockingly. "Why, he just figured one of you boys was about to shoot me in the back. He figured Ben Stowe had put you up to it. How about it, boys? Any of you want me? If you do, you don't need to wait."

His Winchester was in the boot, his slicker was hanging open and loose, and both his hands were in sight.

There were five of them, and they were spread out before him like a hand of cards, all jacks or aces, not a deuce in the lot.

These were hard men, who rode a hard trail in a hard country, and he faced them, waiting. One showdown at a time, he told himself. When I ride up to Tappan Junction, I want to keep my eyes up front.

Billy Daniels moved his hands out in front of him and folded them on his saddlehorn. "The way I see it, you fought beside us back there. You came down off that slope when you didn't need to, and you saved our bacon—some of us, anyway."

"Why, sure!" Al agreed. "That man down there is payin' our wages, but this looks a mite different."

"You want help?" Billy said.

"No help . . . you just leave me ride down there and talk this over with Ben. I mean, we go in with the pack train, but the rest of it is up to Ben and me, and whoever's down there with him."

"Why, that's fair enough," Al commented. "I hear tell Ben Stowe is something to look at with a gun. I'd sort of like to see the cut of the man I'm workin' for."

"Thanks, boys. Bring in the train, will you? But look, stay clear of Ben Stowe and me, and if you see that lady in trouble, give her a hand. She is a lady, boys." He gestured toward the mules. "All that belongs to her, by rights. Bring it in, will you?"

Deliberately, he swung his horse, turning his back on them. And then he cantered out over the darkening prairie.

"You know something?" The Arkansawyer spat. "There goes a square man!"

As Shevlin started across the flat, he paused only to slip out of his slicker and tie it behind his saddle. The clouds were breaking, and a star was showing through. He loosened the Winchester in his boot, singing softly, *"As I walked out on the streets of Laredo, As I walked out in Laredo one day . . ."*

The room was long and low, with a counter doubling as a bar. There were shelves of canned goods, stacked Levis, slickers, and boots. The room smelled of new leather, dry goods, strong coffee, and stronger plug tobacco. Behind the counter sat Tag Murray and the telegrapher, minding their own affairs.

Red, still pale from the abuse he had taken for bringing Laine Tennison to Tappan, clutched a beer in his hand, staring at the circles he was drawing on the bar.

Laine, standing very straight, smiled at Ben. "Really, Mr. Stowe, if you plan to take my gold from here, you must expect trouble. You're going to have to cut telegraph wires, even do some shooting. Your retriever here," she gestured at Red, "did not notice that Doctor Clagg, Billy Townsend, and several others—including Wilson Hoyt—were saddling up when we passed the stable."

"Ma'am," Ben Stowe said abruptly, "you sit down and shut up."

"Now, look here, Ben—" Tag started to protest.

"You shut up, too. Red, put a shotgun on them. If they start anything give them both barrels, then reload and shoot them again."

"Do you really believe," Laine said, "that you will get out of the Territory with that gold? Will it be so easy, Mr. Stowe?"

Ben Stowe's anger was passing. Red had been a damned fool to bring Laine Tennison here, but he needed Red for the time being, and the girl was no more than a nuisance.

"Sorry, Red. I spoke too fast. All we need is a hysterical woman on our hands."

"Sure, Boss. I wasn't thinkin'."

Ben Stowe knew that the rain had stopped, and that the sounds he had been hearing for the last few seconds were those of a walking horse. The first few hoof-falls had barely touched the fringe of his consciousness, but now he was sharply aware that a horse had come to a stop outside.

He half turned to face the door, heard something hit the mud, and then blundering footsteps. The door opened and Babcock came in.

His face was haggard, the wound had started to bleed again, and his shirt was already stiff with dried blood.

"Tag," he said, "I caught a bad one. It's real bad."

Ignoring the shotgun, Tag Murray moved quickly to Babcock's side and eased him into a chair. Laine Tennison, without being asked, had gone to the stove and was pouring hot water into a tin basin. Tag began cutting away the shirt with scissors.

"What happened?" Ben Stowe asked.

When Babcock did not reply, Stowe stepped to the bar and poured a stiff drink of whiskey, and handed it to the wounded man. "What happened?" he asked again.

Babcock tossed off the liquor in two quick gulps. "First drink you ever bought me, Ben. Thanks."

He looked up at Stowe. "When your mule train didn't show up, Winkler figured it out and we cut over the hills. We were set to ambush the train, then that damn' Shevlin came down on us from behind. I never did figure how he got there.

"He was on us before we knew what happened, and his first shot tipped the mule drivers and they came up the slope. Shevlin killed Ray Hollister. Winkler and Sande and Halloran got it, too."

"How many of my men?"

"Three down and a couple scratched."

"Shevlin?"

"He's bringin' the stuff in. He told me to go on ahead an' get Tag here to fix me up."

Ben Stowe looked at the arm with distaste. Used as he was to violence, he never liked to look upon the results of violence, and Babcock's arm was a sorry sight. The bullet must have caught the arm when it was bent and upraised, for it had shattered the elbow, torn the biceps, and imbedded itself in the deltoid muscle at the end of the shoulder.

"We better get Doc Clagg over here, Bab," Murray said. "That's surely a mess. I don't think anybody can make anything of that elbow again."

"Fix it as best you can." Babcock stared bleakly into the years ahead as a one-armed cowman. However, he had seen a few, and some did pretty well. If somebody else could, he could.

"Whatever happens," Ben Stowe said, "you people stay clear of it. I don't want to shoot anybody protecting a legitimate gold shipment.

"That man"—he indicated Babcock—"is an admitted outlaw. He attempted to steal the shipment from the mine of which I am superintendent. Please remember that."

"You are discharged," Laine said, "and you are not authorized to make such a shipment."

Stowe smiled at her. "Now, ma'am," he said pleasantly, "I know you as a guest of Doc Clagg's. Whatever else you may be, I don't know. You've no authority that I know of, and no cause even to be here except that Red here figured I would want to talk to you. He was wrong.

"I am," he went on, speaking clearly, "making a legitimate shipment from the mines of a small amount of gold. I have the authority to do this. If anyone interferes, I shall take legal action."

Laine looked around helplessly. The telegrapher merely shrugged. Tag Murray was busy with Babcock, and Red grinned smugly. Of course, what Stowe said was true. Even if the law had been here, she could not have stopped the shipment . . . not just on her word alone. And the train was due in less than an hour.

Just the same, Ben Stowe was worried. Laine could see it in his restlessness, in his continual glances at the clock. The train was coming soon and the gold had not yet arrived.

And right in the middle of things was Mike Shevlin. He was the key man. He was working for her, but Ben Stowe had offered him a better deal. As for whatever else there was between herself and Shevlin, was there really something there? Or had she only imagined it?

From the first, she had felt drawn to him, less to his undeniable good looks than to his strength. When all the others had wavered, he had stood for what he believed, and down deep within her she was positive that he still stood for it, that he was the man she believed in. Yet the question was there: was he the sort of man she thought, or was she only listening to a wish that he might be?

Red lounged against the counter, a cigarette dangling from his lips, the shotgun in his hands.

Ben Stowe walked over to the window and looked out, but the night was dark, and revealed nothing. When she looked at him, she was shaken with fear for Mike Shevlin. Ben Stowe looked formidable. He was big, powerful, and somehow seemed indomitable. He seemed beyond the strength of the men around her, beyond anyone's strength.

Yet he was gambling now, gambling with his life and the work of years. He was gambling that another man, who was perhaps an enemy, would bring that gold across the mountains. That he had done so was obvious, for Babcock had crossed with Shevlin. Where was Shevlin now? There was no sound in the room except the heavy tick of the clock and the subdued rustling where Tag Murray worked over Babcock.

Suddenly Murray turned and straightened up. "Ben, we've got to send for Doc Clagg. Else this man will lose an arm."

"The hell with him!" Stowe said violently, then he glanced around at Babcock. After all, the issue would have been decided long before Clagg could get here. "Oh, all right," he said with a shrug.

There was a moment of silence in the room, for the question in the mind of each was: Who will go?

Laine looked at Ben Stowe, an amused smile on her lips. "I am sure Red would like to go. Wouldn't you, Red?"

Stowe turned sharply from the window. "Like hell! I need

him right here." He glanced around. "You can go, Tag, or you can wait until my men get here and I'll send one of them. After all, I have five men out there with Shevlin."

"Don't be too sure," Babcock said.

"What's that mean?"

Babcock raised his head and stared at Ben Stowe. "It means those men rode over the mountains with Mike Shevlin, and when they had a fight, Mike pulled them out of it. Mike was with them . . . you weren't. Don't be too damn' sure they're still your men."

"I bought 'em an' paid for 'em," Stowe said contemptuously.

"If you think that, you've come a lot further from the old days than I figured. You can't buy men like that. They work for gun wages, all right, but they ride for the *man*. Right now you're only somebody in an office somewhere. Mike Shevlin is out there sitting his saddle with them. He's rained on when they are, and when they're cold, he is. I can tell you one thing, Ben, if I hadn't got shot up I'd be out there with him right now."

Ben Stowe stayed by the window for a moment longer, then came back to the middle of the room. He went to the counter, where the long bundle that had been behind his saddle lay.

Unrolling it, he took out two double-barreled shotguns, Express guns. Coolly, he loaded them. Beside the bundle lay his Winchester and he took it up, checking to see if there was a cartridge in position.

Nobody spoke, they simply watched him; and he ignored them, as if they did not exist. Indeed, Laine decided, they did not exist for him, for he was wholly concentrated on what was to come; she could see it in his every movement. He was pointed, even as one of his guns would be pointed, toward the moment of decision.

But the moment did not come.

The minutes ticked by, and suddenly Laine noticed that Stowe was perspiring—the sweat stood out in beads on his forehead. A slight sound came from outside, and Stowe turned sharply. Something rattled on the roof.

Suddenly, several horses passed by, moving swiftly. Outside, somebody laughed, and it was a shocking sound to those in the room.

Several minutes of stillness passed, and then a door slammed. The telegrapher looked up. "That was my door," he said, and added, glancing slyly at Stowe, "I wonder if any of those men can use a telegraph key? That Shevlin now, he's been around."

"Don't be a fool!" Stowe said sharply. "I've known him since he was a kid."

"You mean you knew him *when* he was a kid," Babcock said, "but that man's covered a lot of country since then. You don't know a damn' thing about him!"

The real question in Stowe's mind was: Where was the gold at this moment? Had it been loaded into the waiting car?

He swept the room with a quick glance. "All right, Red. I'm going out there. You keep these people sitting just where they are.

"Babcock, I'll send one of my men for Doc Clagg. I'll see no man suffer, and we shared a blanket a couple of times in the old days."

He looked from one man to another. "Every move I've made in arranging this shipment has been legal," he said. "I wouldn't want anybody to try stopping me now. I'd have every right to suspect them of trying to steal company gold."

He moved to the door and stepped outside.

TWENTY-ONE

The clouds had broken and the stars were out, but water still dripped from the eaves of the railroad station and Murray's Saloon at Tappan Junction.

At the hitch rail stood half a dozen horses with empty saddles, and another horse had just come down from the mountains, riderless since the afternoon's shooting. It stood now, bridle trailing, close beside the tied horses.

Light from the saloon windows fell across the wet platform outside, across the glistening steel rails, and almost met through the darkness the light from the telegraph station windows. Beyond those windows one of the men was brewing a fresh pot of coffee in the operator's pot, which they had quickly emptied.

Mike Shevlin, leaning against the corner of the loading pens near the chute, saw Ben Stowe come outside. His right arm was straight down by his side, which meant that he was carrying a weapon close against him where it could not be easily seen. Mike, who knew all the subterfuges, watched thoughtfully.

Ben was looking around warily. He was like an old grizzly that senses trouble, but has failed to locate it. Suddenly he stepped off the platform and strode across the tracks to the station.

When Stowe opened the door, Mike could hear his voice. "Where's Shevlin?"

The reply was muffled, then Stowe spoke again. "All right. I'm payin' you boys top wages—let's go get him!"

Evidently one of the men had come to the door, for the words were plain—it sounded like Billy Daniels.

"We'd like to see you go get him yourself. There's only one of him, and he's right around close."

"So it's like that, is it? Well, you're fired—every last one of you! Now take yourselves out of here!"

"We like it here," Al's voice drawled. "We're stayin' on for the show. We got us gallery seats."

Ben Stowe turned away without speaking, then he halted. "Look," he said, "Babcock needs Doc Clagg or he'll lose an arm. One of you boys ride after him, will you?"

There was a moment of silence, and then one of the men detached himself from the group. "I'll go. I'll see no man lose an arm if I can help it."

Ben Stowe walked to the middle of the tracks and stopped there, waiting until the hoof-beats died away in the distance.

Now, just where would Shevlin be? At the pens? Or at the car where the gold should be? Probably at the car. He took a moment longer to get his eyes accustomed to the darkness, and then he walked along the track.

Mike Shevlin knew every thought that was going through Stowe's head. He knew what he was thinking, because he knew what he himself would be thinking at such a time.

Far away, he heard a distant echoing sound—the train whistle. It was going to be as close as that.

Mike Shevlin rolled the dead cigar in his teeth and looked toward the dark figure of the big man coming toward him. *Well, Ben, it's been a long time coming. Did you ever figure it would be like this? Just you and me in the black, wet night?*

There had been neither saloon or station here in the early days—only the stock pens and the loading chute. They had loaded Rafter cattle from here . . . how many times?

Ben Stowe stepped aside suddenly and disappeared. Mike held himself very still.

Now what? Had Stowe just stepped aside and crouched down in the blackness; or was he coming on along beside the track? He was out of range of the lights, and probably was in the shallow ditch alongside the roadbed.

Suddenly cold steel touched Shevlin lightly behind the ear, and a cool voice said, "I could let him kill you, but it's easier this way."

Clagg Merriam!

Mike Shevlin had one boot on the lowest bar of the pen, and as that voice spoke, he threw himself back, shoving hard with his boot.

He staggered the man behind him, and a shot bellowed right alongside Mike's ear. They hit the ground together, and instantly Shevlin threw himself clear, rolled into the ditch, and scrambled under the loading chute.

Ben Stowe, believing he had been shot at, shot quickly; and almost with the sound of the second shot, a rifle bellowed from the top of a cattle car, and a bullet struck sparks from a rail near where Ben lay.

"What the hell's goin' on?" shouted a voice from the station.

Mike Shevlin held himself tight against the lowest part of the loading chute, partly protected by the posts of its underpinning. Clagg Merriam was out there . . . and the other one with the rifle—that must be Burt Parry.

Why hadn't Merriam simply fired, instead of opening his mouth? And Parry should have held his fire until he had Ben Stowe outlined. It would have been simple enough, with a little patience.

A cold drop of water fell on Shevlin's head behind the ear and trickled slowly down his neck and under his shirt. His leg was cramping but he waited, holding his six-shooter ready.

Suddenly, from behind the stock pens, Ben Stowe shouted, "Mike! Let's get 'em! They butted into a private fight!"

Just then a gun flashed and a bullet spat slivers into Mike's face—a gun not a dozen feet away. He lunged from his cover, firing as he went, and he heard the *thud* of a bullet's impact on flesh, and a muffled grunt.

Again a gun flashed, but this time it was not pointed at him, and he shot into the dark figure as he ran by with a bullet whipping past his face.

He lifted his pistol to fire again, and as he did so two guns barked, almost together. The first was Merriam's, wounded but not dead; the other was Ben Stowe's almost instant reply.

Shevlin heard a gun fall into the cinders, and then he thrust his hand into the cattle car and triggered three fast, spaced shots through the roof of the car where Burt Parry was lying.

Parry screamed, and at the sound Stowe, who had climbed one of the cars, fired. The body slid from the top of the car and fell to the roadbed near where Shevlin was standing.

"Ben!" he called.

"You're talkin'!"

"We got 'em both. Now you get on that train and get out of here."

"You'd like that, wouldn't you?" Suddenly Ben's voice changed. "Like hell I will! I'll see you dead first!"

"Ben . . . one thing—*who killed Eli?*"

"*I* did, you damn' fool! Merriam thought he did. They were arguing, and I saw Clagg was gettin' nowhere, so when Merriam shot and missed, I killed Eli—from my office window."

Mike tugged off one boot, then the other. He was wearing

thick woollen socks. He felt sure that Ben was creeping closer, for the sound of those last words had been nearby and close to the ground. Ben had been shooting a pistol, but he still had a shotgun or a rifle . . . at this distance those shotgun slugs would cut a man in two.

Suddenly Ben Stowe spoke. "You can still cut out, Mike. You don't need to die."

How far away was he now? Maybe twenty paces. And Ben was without doubt in shelter of some kind, waiting for Mike's reply, to cut him in two.

Turning quickly, Mike ran back along the track, his socks making no sound on the wooden cross-ties. He heard the train, closer now, whistling for the station. Leaping to clear the cinders of the roadbed, he landed close against the pens, then with a swift lunge he rounded the corner.

The headlight of the train was shining off across the flat, for the train had not yet rounded the bend toward the station. When the locomotive rounded the bend, the headlight would throw the whole area into sharp relief.

The train whistled again, and then the light swung as the engine came around the bend. There was Ben Stowe, standing squarely in the middle of the track, the shotgun in his hands, waiting for that glare of light.

They saw each other at the same instant—or maybe Mike had a bit the best of it, for he was not where Ben Stowe might have expected him to be. The shotgun came up and Mike fired. Slugs ripped through the air around him, something tugged at his pants. He stepped forward and shot again, and Ben Stowe went down to his hands and knees. The train was thundering down upon him, and Mike rushed forward in a desperate lunge, jerking Stowe free of the tracks with only seconds to spare.

The train roared by within inches of them, then Ben Stowe came up on his knees, a Colt gripped in his fist. "Thanks, Mike!" he yelled, and fired.

Shevlin felt the shock of the bullet, and he knew he had dropped his gun. He had reloaded behind the stock pens, and there were still one or two—

Stowe was resting his gun across a forearm for dead aim, so Mike Shevlin drew Hollister's gun from his waistband and as he swung it around he fired three shots as fast as he could make them roll.

Stowe fired once. The bullet missed, struck the steel rail, and ricocheted off into the night with a nasty whine.

Mike caught hold of the rail and pulled himself around. He

was conscious that men had gotten down from the train and others had come up on horseback, but he was concentrating on one thing only: he had to get Bén Stowe.

He twisted around to look at Stowe. Ben's face was bloody, and his shirt was dark with blood.

"You got me," he gasped. "You always were shot with luck!" Even as he spoke, he brought his gun up with startling speed, and Mike shot into him again.

Then there was only silence, the hiss of steam from the engine, and, after a moment, a mutter of excited voices and a shuffling of feet.

Someone was kneeling over Shevlin. It was Doc Clagg. "Babcock," Mike said, "he's hurt bad, you—"

But he was keeping his eyes on Ben Stowe, clutching his empty gun and waiting for him to move. Only Ben did not move, and never would again.

"He said I was shot with luck," Mike said slowly. "I wish that was all he had in those guns."

"You'll live," Doc Clagg assured him grimly. "Your kind are too tough to die."

The cattle business around Rafter never recovered, and after the mines played out Rafter became a ghost town. Mike and Laine Shevlin never did live there, for they moved to California when he was able to travel. Shevlin ran cattle there for quite a few years.

Thirty years ago they ripped up the long-unused tracks that had been the only excuse for Tappan Junction. The buildings were destroyed when a tourist dropped a cigarette from his car as it raced along the highway that had been built at the foot of the mountains.

Laine Shevlin lived to a fine old age until one of her grandsons became an ad man on Madison Avenue; after that there wasn't much to live for. She just wasted away, and after Mike saw her buried he walked out of the cemetery and disappeared.

There was quite a lot of talk, and the newspapers dug up the fact that he had been a Texas Ranger and something of a gunfighter, reprinting some of the old stories, with some confusion as to names and dates.

The only one who could have offered a clue was the last of the old-timers. He had taken to sitting on a bench in the sun alongside a filling station on the new highway, and he was there when the car pulled up and the tall old man called over to him.

"Wasn't there a place called Tappan Junction somewhere about here?"

The old-timer peered toward the driver. "Hey? Did you say Tappan Junction? She used to lie right out there on the flat."

The sitter's pipe had gone out and he fumbled in his pockets for a match. "Young folks, they ain't never heard of Tappan."

"What about Stone Cabin?" the man in the car asked.

"Stone Cabin?" Through the fog of years the words startled the old man. "Did you say *Stone Cabin?*"

When old Mike Shevlin turned up missing he was still a wealthy man, and there was quite a search for him. The highway police made inquiries, and at the filling station the old-timer was pointed out to them.

"Doubt if he can he'p you much," the station attendant said. "He's almost lost his sight, and that one arm, that's been no good for years. Horse fell on it, I guess, a good many years back. Why, that old feller's nigh to a hundred years old! Ninety-odd, anyway."

They asked their questions after they found Mike Shevlin's car abandoned in a cove at the foot of the mountains, but the old man did not pay much attention. Only after they had turned away did he mutter to himself as he sat there.

"Tappan Junction . . . Stone Cabin . . . that's been a while. 'You tell Doc Clagg,' he said, 'you tell Doc Clagg I ain't as tough as I used to be.' "

"Stone Cabin?" the attendant repeated in answer to their query. "Never heard of it. I've lived around here more'n ten years, and I never heard the name."

The officer looked at the high green hills, rolling back in somber magnificence, wild and lonely. They told him nothing.

"What's back up there?" he asked.

"Nothin'. There ain't no road. Ain't been anybody back in there that I can remember. Folks don't stop here for more'n gas and the time of day. They just breeze on through. We hereabouts, we got no time for lookin' in the mountains."

It was forty miles back to the highway police office, and they could just make it by quitting time.

As they were driving back the officer looked at his companion. "Didn't you tell me your folks came from this part of the country?"

"My granddaddy did. But he never talked about it, or else I didn't listen. Anyway, I don't believe it was as rough as they say. His name was the same as mine . . . Wilson Hoyt."

They settled back and listened to the hum of the motor and the sound of the tires, and watched the windshield wiper, for it was beginning to rain.

It was raining, too, up at Stone Cabin, just as it had long ago.